"Julie, the man who phoned was just some crazy person," Chase said

"Honest, Daddy?"

"Yes…" He waited, suspecting his daughter wasn't quite done.

Sure enough, she said, "Anne was just gonna tell me how we could stop the police from thinking Aunt Rachel killed Graham."

"You told Anne that Rachel is the *girlfriend* the reporters are referring to?"

"No, just that I knew somebody with a problem…."

"Julie, why did you think you should talk to Anne about this?"

"Because she knows all about what the police do. When Penelope Snow figures things out in Anne's books, that's only make-believe. Really it's Anne."

"I know, baby. But when she makes up a story she puts in details that all fit together. That doesn't mean she can figure out a real-life mystery."

"Yes, she can. 'Cuz she used to be a private detective. She told me her father's one, too."

"Really," he said again, his brain shifting gears. Here he was, not knowing what on earth he should do, and he'd suddenly acquired a neighbor who might be able to give him some advice. "Julie? Do you think it would be okay if I went back over and talked to Anne with you?"

Dear Reader,

Close Neighbors is a story about relationships, not only the developing romantic one between Anne Barrett and Chase Nicholson, but also the long-established ones in Anne's and Chase's families—particularly between Chase's nine-year-old daughter, Julie, and the significant adults in her life.

The book spans a short period of time, yet each of these relationships evolves during the story. Most of us find change frightening, but as Julie's grandmother tells her, "Darling, if everything always stayed the same, life would be awfully boring."

I think it's safe to say that *Close Neighbors* is anything but boring.

This book is special to me because my father helped me plot a good deal of it while he was in the hospital. That gave me a wonderful head start when it came to the actual writing, so if you ever find yourself spending a lot of time visiting someone in the hospital, you might consider trying your hand at a book. In the meanwhile, I hope you enjoy *Close Neighbors*.

Warmest,

Dawn Stewardson

CLOSE NEIGHBORS
Dawn Stewardson

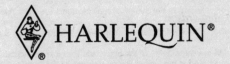

HARLEQUIN®

TORONTO • NEW YORK • LONDON
AMSTERDAM • PARIS • SYDNEY • HAMBURG
STOCKHOLM • ATHENS • TOKYO • MILAN • MADRID
PRAGUE • WARSAW • BUDAPEST • AUCKLAND

ISBN 0-373-70909-9

CLOSE NEIGHBORS

Copyright © 2000 by Dawn Stewardson.

This edition published by arrangement with Harlequin Books S.A.

® and TM are trademarks of the publisher. Trademarks indicated with
® are registered in the United States Patent and Trademark Office, the
Canadian Trade Marks Office and in other countries.

Visit us at www.eHarlequin.com

Printed in U.S.A.

This one is for my father,
who spent countless hours helping me with the plotting.

And for John, always.

PROLOGUE

"THERE. ALL DONE." Julie set a third glass of water on the table and smiled, then felt awful when Aunt Rachel didn't smile back.

She hadn't smiled all day. In fact, she'd been crying earlier. She'd come out of her room with her eyes red and her face puffy. So even though both she and Daddy kept saying there was no reason to be worried, Julie knew there was.

They'd kind of fooled her this morning, when they'd sat her down and explained what had happened. They'd made it sound okay.

Well, *okay* wasn't exactly right. If you knew somebody and he got killed, it was probably never okay. But they'd said it was just one of those unfortunate things, so she hadn't really been afraid. Not until the police detectives arrived.

That had been scary. And the stuff on TV was even worse.

At first, Daddy wasn't going to let her watch it. Then he'd decided she'd see it at a friend's house or something, anyway, and it would be better if she watched with them—so they could explain what was true and what wasn't.

It was the stuff that wasn't true that had been really bad. 'Cuz even though the newspeople never said Rachel's name, they kept talking about an ex-girlfriend being the last person to see Graham alive—except for the killer. Only, somehow, they made it sound as if the police thought Rachel was the killer.

Daddy'd said they just did things like that so people would watch *their* news instead of somebody else's. But when they made it sound like your aunt was a murderer, you felt awful.

"Hon?" Rachel glanced at her, then dropped a handful of spaghetti into the boiling water. "Would you go tell your dad that dinner's in ten minutes?"

"Sure."

She headed out of the kitchen and started up the backstairs. Her friends thought it was funny that their house had an extra set of stairs. But after her mom left, Daddy built a big addition across the back—so they'd have a family room downstairs and his office upstairs—and he'd put in the second staircase.

That was way before she'd started school, and he'd wanted the office so he could work at home more. Then, after her aunt moved in, one of them was almost always home. Rachel only worked when she had an assignment taking pictures to go with a magazine article or something.

Just as Julie reached the upstairs hall, the office phone began ringing. That meant she'd have to make one of those throat-cutting signs to her dad, 'cuz Rachel hated when the spaghetti got cooked too long, and—

"You're insane!"

Daddy's words froze her before she reached the

doorway. He sounded angry, but kind of afraid, too, and he was never afraid.

Listening in on someone else's conversation was against the rules, but she stayed right where she was, barely breathing.

"Of course I know they haven't found it."

Her heart had begun thumping, and she half wanted to run back down the stairs, half wanted to stay and hear more.

"You're out of your mind! She didn't kill him, so her fingerprints can't be on it."

The words *kill* and *fingerprints* started a hot, prickly feeling in her chest. She wished she'd decided to run back downstairs, because she was getting so scared that she felt like hiding in her closet, the way she used to when she was real little.

"You bastard! We'll see what the cops think about that!"

Her eyes began to sting with tears. Daddy *never* swore. Maybe *hell* or *dammit*, sometimes, but never anything worse.

"Oh? And if I *do* call them? Are you going to walk into police headquarters with that gun? Don't you think they'd have the brains to—"

One Mississippi, two Mississippi, three Mississippi, she silently counted. How many seconds would it take for Daddy to hear what would happen if he called the cops?

She kept counting and counting but never found out.

The next thing she heard was the little beep his cordless made when you clicked it off.

CHAPTER ONE

"SWANSEA, SWANSEA, how I love ya, how I love ya…"

Her song dissolving into laughter, Anne stepped out of the shower and grabbed a towel. She was such a dreadful singer that anyone hearing her would take off running. This morning, though, she felt so good she doubted it would bother her.

Rather than having to sleep through the rumble of streetcars and honking horns in downtown last night, she'd been treated to silence. And she'd awakened to the twitter of birds.

Thus far, she thought, searching through a carton labeled Shorts & Stuff, not a single one of her brand-new-home-owner fears had become a reality. And even though she'd barely moved in, she was already starting to think her real estate agent had told her the truth. That she'd never regret buying in the peaceful west-end neighborhood of Swansea.

Of course, only yesterday morning, some dog walker had discovered a body in nearby High Park— the body of a police detective, no less. She'd heard about it on the news last night, while she'd been making sure her clock radio had survived the move.

But murders were uncommon in Toronto, especially in tony areas like the High Park district.

After finally finding a T-shirt that wasn't too wrinkled, she pulled it on and headed downstairs. There, the mountains of boxes seemed to have multiplied overnight. But even that wasn't enough to dampen her mood.

She started the coffee brewing, spent a few minutes searching for her laptop, then carried it and a mug of coffee out to the patio table.

Some of the friends who'd helped her move had offered to come back today. And her father had downright insisted. But she'd convinced even him that she wanted to spend the first day in her new home alone.

And now that it had turned out to be so gorgeous…well, there was just no way she could waste a July-perfect morning unpacking. Not when she had such a terrific idea for her next book that she was positively itching to get started.

While the computer ran its warm-up checks, she sat happily contemplating her new little corner of the world—bright sky above, light breeze rustling the leaves of her twin aspens, the pool's water sparkling with diamonds, and…someone spying on her.

A vaguely uneasy feeling stole up her spine. She'd never had much in the way of woman's intuition, but she did have a sixth sense that warned her when she was being watched.

Hoping someone was merely curious about the new neighbor, she slowly scanned the length of the cedar privacy fence—seeing no one, yet certain someone was there. A couple of seconds later she heard a quiet creak, and the gate to the yard backing onto hers opened a few inches.

A girl of eight or nine peered tentatively over at her, a skinny little thing with long, pale hair.

"Hi." Anne shot her a smile. "Are you my neighbor?"

The child nodded solemnly.

"Well, I'm Anne. And you're…?"

"Julie."

"That's a pretty name."

"Thanks. It's really Juliette, but nobody ever calls me that."

"Ah. Do you wish people would?"

When the girl simply shrugged, then stood looking uncertain, Anne nodded toward her mug. "I guess you're a little young for coffee?"

"I tried it once, but I didn't like it."

"Well, I've got orange juice in the fridge. How about some of that?"

"Umm…my dad said I shouldn't bother you."

"You're not. So why don't you come and sit down while I get some juice."

"No, that's okay. I already had my juice. But do you think I could talk to you for a minute?"

"Sure."

Julie closed the gate, then skirted the end of the pool and silently sat down.

"Did you want to talk about anything in particular?" Anne finally prompted.

"Do you really write the Penelope Snow mysteries?"

"Yes, I do."

"I like them. My aunt buys them for me."

"Well, that's good to hear. But how did you know who I was?"

"'Cuz my aunt asked Mrs. Kitchner who our new neighbor was gonna be. That's who lived here before. Mr. and Mrs. Kitchner."

Anne nodded. "I met them the first time I came to look at the house."

"Well, Mrs. Kitchner told Rachel—that's my aunt—what your name was, and said you wrote books for kids. And Rachel knew right away who you were. But when I saw you...you kind of look like the picture on the books, but different."

"I know. I always freeze when there's a camera pointed at me."

"Rachel says lots of people do. She's a photographer. That's what I'm going to be when I grow up."

"You are, eh?"

Julie nodded. "Rachel gave me one of her old cameras and taught me how to do all the settings and everything."

"It sounds as if you and Rachel are pretty close."

"Uh-huh. She lives with me and my dad. 'Cuz my mom and dad are divorced."

Anne hesitated, not sure if she should say that was too bad.

Before she could decide, Julie added, "My mom's

a singer. And she lives in Los Angeles now, 'cuz it's where the best jobs are.''

"Ah." She left it at that, although she couldn't help wondering what kind of woman would move thousands of miles away from her child.

"Under your picture on the books?" Julie said. "It says you used to be a private eye."

"Uh-huh. That's what my father is, and I used to work for him—until I discovered that writing books was more fun."

"But it's 'cuz you were a detective that you know how to solve mysteries, right? I mean, you pretend it's Penelope who figures everything out, but it's really you."

"Exactly. That's the way writing books works."

"So…you could probably figure out just about anything."

"Well, I wouldn't go as far as *anything,* but…is there something you thought I could help you figure out?"

Julie hesitated, then nodded. "I know someone who has a big problem."

"Oh." The infamous "friend with a problem." Anne resisted the temptation to smile. Whatever was troubling Julie, she obviously believed it was serious.

"So, if I tell you about it, will you figure out what she should do?"

"I'll certainly try."

"Promise?"

"Promise."

The girl gave her a wan smile, then said, "What happened is—"

"Julie?" a man called.

"That's my dad!" she whispered fiercely. "Don't tell him what I was saying, okay?"

"Okay," Anne said, glancing over at Julie's father.

He was tall, his head and shoulders visible above the fence, and she quickly appraised what she could see of him.

In his mid-thirties, he wasn't handsome in a conventional way. His nose was a bit too large, his dark hair longish and decidedly unruly, his eyebrows on the thick side. Still, he was the kind of man who seemed comfortable in his own skin, and there was something more than a little attractive about him.

"Hi," he said, reaching the fence. "I'm Chase Nicholson."

"Anne Barrett," she told him—thinking he seemed distracted. But he'd probably been wondering where his daughter was.

"Welcome to the neighborhood." He smiled, and when he did she had a feeling she was going to like him.

"It looks as if you were trying to get some work done," he added, glancing first at her laptop, then at Julie.

"Oh, I hadn't really gotten started, so a little company was fine."

"Good. But I need her to help me with something."

"Right now?" Julie asked.

"Uh-huh. We've got a deadline looming, remember?"

"My dad designs stuff, and I sometimes help," she explained.

Anne glanced at Chase again. "What kind of stuff?"

"Office buildings, mostly. I'm an industrial architect."

"And he has to make models of the buildings," Julie said. "That's what I help with, 'cuz he's got big fingers and for parts of them you need little fingers."

She pushed her chair away from the table, then whispered, "Can I come over again? After I finish helping my dad?"

"Sure you can," Anne whispered back. She could hardly say no, although she suspected it would have been the wiser answer.

Things didn't always occur to her right off the bat, which was one reason she hadn't been a first-rate P.I. And it hadn't struck her, until after she'd promised to try to help, that the adults in Julie's life might not like her turning to a stranger for advice.

Chase opened the gate, and while he waited for Julie to make her way across the yard he did his best to keep his gaze from wandering back to Anne Barrett.

A month or so ago, when Rachel had learned who'd bought the Kitchner house—and that she'd be moving in *alone*—she'd shown him Anne's photo on the back of one of Julie's books. To say it didn't do her justice was an understatement.

Her dark hair, longer and shaggier than in the picture, framed a face with high cheekbones, big brown eyes, a cute little nose and the sort of lush lips some women acquired through collagen injections.

She didn't seem the sort who'd do that, though. She was more the casual, natural type. The type he liked.

He mentally shook his head, surprised that thought had even crossed his mind. In the past twenty-four hours, he'd discovered that when you had a sister at risk of being arrested for murder, and an extortionist breathing down your neck, you didn't think about much else.

"WE'LL HAVE TO BE QUIET," Chase told Julie as they started up the backstairs. "Rachel's lying down."

"Has she got one of her migraines?"

"The beginnings of one. She didn't sleep well last night."

"'Cuz she was too worried, right?"

He nodded. His daughter was no dummy, and now that she'd realized Rachel might be in serious trouble there was little point in trying to convince her otherwise.

They headed into his office, where the half-put-together model sat waiting for them. Initially, he'd only begun asking for Julie's help as a way of spending more time with her, but her little fingers actually did make the jobs easier. And she generally concentrated so hard that she didn't talk much, which was exactly what he needed today.

As long as he had silence, working with his hands helped him think—and he sure had to do some more thinking about that phone call.

When he'd hung up, he'd simply intended to tell Rachel about it, then call those detectives. But he hadn't gone beyond step one, because she'd had a fit at the idea of telling the police. And while she'd made a convincing case against it, he wasn't sure they'd come to the right decision.

Of course, if he called now, the cops would figure it was strange that he'd waited until today to phone them. But if he didn't do that, what the hell *should* he do?

"Aren't we gonna get started?" Julie asked.

"Uh-huh, I was just thinking about which section we'd work on first." He reached for a tube of glue.

"Dad?" she said as he opened it.

"What?"

"Do the police *really* think Rachel killed Graham? Like all those reporters are saying?"

He slowly screwed the cap back onto the tube, searching for the right words.

"First off," he finally said, "that isn't exactly what the reporters are saying. They're only suggesting it's what the police *might* be thinking. And as I told you yesterday, they speculate about a lot of things when they shouldn't."

"But if the police *don't* think it, then how come those detectives were here for so long yesterday?"

"Because they had to go over every detail of what happened the other night. Maybe something Graham said or something Rachel noticed will help them with the case."

"But they were here *forever*."

"Well, I think they're probably even more thorough than usual when someone on the police force has been killed."

Julie nodded slowly. That was something else scary. Graham knew all about bad people 'cuz he'd been a police detective. So if he could get killed, then anybody could.

She looked at her dad again, thinking he hadn't exactly answered her question. "But they *might* be thinking Rachel killed him?"

"Darling…they didn't tell her that she was under suspicion. And they didn't say so when they talked to me, either."

"But—"

"Baby, everything's going to be just fine. Because she had nothing to do with it."

"I know, but…" Julie paused, still not sure whether to tell Daddy she'd heard him on the phone. Or what she'd been talking to Anne Barrett about.

When she'd seen Anne sitting in her yard, she'd right away thought that going over and asking her for advice was a great idea. That Anne would know how they could make the police see Rachel hadn't had anything to do with Graham getting killed.

But now she was thinking how Daddy always said not to talk about family stuff outside the house. So maybe she shouldn't say she was going next door again until after she'd already been. 'Cuz once Anne told her what they should do to help Rachel, Daddy wouldn't be mad.

Or maybe he would. She'd still have been talking about family stuff to a stranger.

Rats. She just didn't know what to do.

"Julie? Why don't you tell me exactly what you're afraid is going to happen, okay?"

She swallowed hard. Sometimes her dad could read her mind, and she was pretty sure he was doing it right now.

"I'm…I'm mostly afraid they'll put Rachel in jail."

"I see. Baby, do you understand what circumstantial evidence is?"

"Uh-uh."

"Well, it's not like someone saying he saw who shot Graham. If anyone had, the police would know Rachel didn't do it.

"But there wasn't an eyewitness. And the fact she was with him before he was killed is one of the *circumstances* in the case. So it's called circumstantial evidence. And because she was with him, the police have to consider the possibility she might have done it. You follow?"

"I guess. But…Daddy…" She took a deep breath, then let the words tumble out. "I heard you on the phone last night. What you said about fingerprints? And about calling the cops?"

Chase swore to himself.

"I didn't listen on purpose. I was only coming to tell you dinner was ready."

"Julie, don't worry about what you heard, okay? After dinner, Rachel and I talked about it and decided the man who phoned was just some crazy person."

"Honest?"

"Yes. So you do your best to forget about it. It didn't mean anything." He waited, certain his daughter wasn't done quite yet.

Sure enough, she said, "When you came looking for me? When I was next door?"

"Uh-huh?"

"Anne was just gonna tell me how we could stop the police from thinking Rachel killed Graham."

Chase simply stared at Julie. If she'd told Anne Barrett that she'd moved in next door to a murder suspect... It was hardly the sort of news flash that would make the woman's day—to say the least.

"You told Anne that Rachel is the *girlfriend* the reporters are referring to?" he said at last.

"No, I didn't get that far. I only got to saying I knew somebody with a problem. And Anne said she'd help me figure out what to do about it. But then you said I had to help you."

Thank heavens for good timing.

"She said I could come back later, though."

"Julie...I'm not clear on why you thought you should talk to Anne about this."

"Because she knows all about what the police do. And about mysteries and stuff. When Penelope Snow figures things out in the books, that's only make-believe. Really, it's Anne.''

"I know, baby. But she doesn't exactly figure things out. When she makes up a story, she puts in details that all fit together—so it *seems* as if Penelope Snow solves a mystery. That doesn't mean Anne could figure out a real-life one.''

"Yes, she could. 'Cuz she used to be a private detective.''

Chase shook his head.

"She did! It says on her books. Right under her picture. I can show you.''

"No, it's okay. Now that you're saying so, I remember it does. But you can't believe everything you read. No more than you can believe everything those TV reporters say.''

"But she *was* one,'' Julie insisted. "She told me.''

"Really?''

"Uh-huh.''

"Are you sure she wasn't just pretending?''

"Uh-huh. She told me her father's one and she used to work for him. Only, then she decided she liked writing books better.''

"Really,'' he said again, his brain shifting gears.

Here he was, not knowing what on earth he should do, and he'd suddenly acquired a neighbor who might be able to give him some advice.

She was like a gift from fate. And even though he'd never normally impose on a woman he barely knew, these were hardly normal circumstances.

Surreptitiously, he glanced at Julie. He didn't want

her any more involved in this than she already was. Yet he could hardly tell her to stay here while he went and talked to Anne without her. Not when, if she hadn't gone over there in the first place…

Deciding he'd just have to play things by ear, and send her home at the first opportune moment, he said, "Julie? Do you think it would be okay if I went back over and talked to Anne with you?"

ANNE HAD BEEN SURE that Julie would reappear, but she hadn't expected it to be this soon. She'd barely gotten started on the opening scene of her book before the girl came through the gate again—her father in tow.

Closing her laptop, she manufactured a smile.

"This time you *were* trying to get some work done," Chase said as they sat down. "So I apologize for bothering you. But Julie tells me you used to be a P.I. And since the problem she wanted to ask you about is a family matter, I thought, if you don't mind my sitting in…"

"No, of course not," she lied. In truth, the idea made her very uncomfortable.

Having a child ask for advice was one thing. Adding her father to the mix was something else entirely. Besides which, she'd assumed Julie wanted to talk about some little-girl issue, not an adult-serious problem.

"Thanks," he said. "I really appreciate that," he added, giving her such an engaging smile she decided she only felt *marginally* uncomfortable.

"Why don't you pick up where you left off," he suggested to Julie.

She nodded, then looked across the table and gnawed on her lower lip for a few seconds. "Have you seen on TV about the man who got killed in High Park?" she finally asked.

"No, my TV's not hooked up yet. But I heard something about it on the radio last night." Surely, though, their problem didn't have anything to do with that. "He was a police detective, wasn't he?"

"Uh-huh. And he used to be my aunt Rachel's boyfriend."

"Really." She tried not to sound surprised.

"Rachel broke up with him less than a week ago," Chase added.

"And the TV people keep talking about her," Julie added. "I mean, they don't say her name. They only call her his ex-girlfriend. But it's her. And they're making it sound like the police think she killed him. And yesterday, two police detectives came to talk to her and my dad. And they had a million questions for both of you. Right, Dad?"

"Right."

"Why you?" Anne asked him.

"Because Rachel was with Graham for a while on Wednesday evening. And, basically, they wanted my recollection about what time she left and came home."

"'Cuz they don't believe what *she* told them," Julie said. "That's why she's afraid."

"Julie—"

"Daddy, she *is*. I can tell." The girl focused on Anne again. "And I thought you'd know how to make them see she'd never kill anyone."

Anne looked at Chase once more.

His gaze flickered to his daughter. Then he nodded almost imperceptibly toward their house.

She began breathing more easily. Clearly, she wasn't the only one who didn't want to say another word about this in front of Julie.

"So...making the police see that someone's innocent," she said to the girl. "That sort of thing always needs some thinking time.

"I assume the detectives gave you the standard warning?" she continued, turning toward Chase. "Told you you're only allowed to discuss what you talked to them about with a lawyer? Or a private investigator?" she added pointedly.

"It's a good thing you reminded me," he said, a relieved expression crossing his face.

"But Anne *is* a private investigator," Julie told him. "At least, she *was*. Doesn't that count, Anne?"

"Yes, it does. But I'm afraid it means your dad won't be able to tell me about that conversation in front of you."

"But...that's not fair!"

"Baby, you wouldn't want me to get into trouble, would you?"

"N-o-o, but—"

"Then how about if you go home. And after I finish talking to Anne, I'll tell you what she thinks."

"Oh, D-a-a-d."

Chase gave her an exaggerated shrug. "There's no other way, Julie. Besides, it's time somebody looked in on Rachel. You could see if she'd like some tea or something."

With obvious reluctance, the child pushed back her chair.

"Julie?" Anne said. "Do you want to come back after lunch? For a swim?"

She glanced at her father. When he nodded, she shot Anne a small smile. "Sure. Thanks."

"See you later, then."

"That was nice of you," Chase said as Julie started across the yard.

"Well, I'll want a swim, anyway, and she's a real sweetheart. I'm just afraid she's going to be disappointed in me. No matter how much thinking I do, I doubt I'll figure out a way of convincing the police about Rachel."

"I know. Hoping you would wasn't one of her more realistic expectations. But there's a different problem that *I* wanted to ask you about."

"Oh?"

He nodded. "Something happened last night that I'm not sure how to handle. A man called me, claiming to have the gun that killed Graham Lowe. He told me it's mine for two hundred thousand bucks. Otherwise, he'll use it to pin the murder on Rachel."

CHAPTER TWO

HOW ON EARTH, ANNE ASKED herself, had things escalated so rapidly from a little girl seeking her advice to a man needing it? And not just *any* man, but one who'd become the victim of an extortion attempt because his sister was a murder suspect.

She gazed across the sun-drenched pool, thinking that when the Nicholsons had a problem it was certainly a major leaguer. And regardless of whether it made her uncomfortable, now that Chase had begun talking about it she had little choice but to hear him out.

"So," she said, turning toward him with what she hoped was an encouraging expression. "When you said you're not sure how to handle the phone call, does that mean you haven't reported it to the police?"

"No. I haven't."

"Then I guess my first question is, why not?"

Silence stretched between them until he said, "You know, all of a sudden I'm feeling like an idiot—and wondering what the devil possessed me to come over here. I mean, we've barely met, so..."

She simply waited, watching him. On the surface, he appeared relaxed, his hands resting lightly on his thighs, but no one looking closely would mistake him for a man at ease. His dark eyes were clouded with worry, and there was a tightness around his mouth.

"When Julie said you'd been a detective..." he finally continued. "But, no. I should have realized that imposing on you was totally inappropriate." He began to rise. "This doesn't concern you, and—"

"Wait, it's all right," she said, aware as the words came out that she might regret them.

Giving advice to a virtual stranger could be risky business, so she'd probably be wiser to just let him leave. But something about him made her want to help.

Before she could decide exactly what it was, he said, "You're sure it's okay?"

"Yes."

He lowered himself into the chair again, slowly saying, "I *would* have called the police, but the situation's a lot more complicated than Julie made it sound."

"In that case, you'd better start at the beginning. Tell me the whole story. I've got time," she added when he glanced at her laptop. "I was just playing with the opening of a new book. And that was mostly because my house is such a disaster area that I don't know where to start attacking it."

"Well...then how about this? After we're finished discussing my problem, I'll give you a hand inside. Help you arrange your furniture, or cart boxes to the basement or whatever."

Her gaze slipped downward from his face. His

shoulders were broad, and the way his T-shirt was pulling tautly across his chest emphasized its muscles, leaving little doubt that he'd be a big help.

"All right." She shot him a smile. "Deal."

"Great. Then…the beginning would have been Wednesday evening. Graham phoned Rachel after dinner and… I mentioned that she'd recently broken up with him, didn't I?"

"Yes."

"Okay. Well, on Wednesday he phoned after dinner and told her they had to talk—suggested they meet in High Park. She said she'd be there, then had second thoughts and called him back. She couldn't reach him, though, so she asked me to go with her.

"It wouldn't have been any problem. Julie was spending the night next door, at her friend's. But Rachel has a habit of avoiding difficult situations, of always trying to get someone else to take care of them for her. So I said no, and she went alone."

When Chase paused and caught Anne's gaze, she felt a flicker of affinity. How often had she made a spur-of-the-moment decision, only to end up wishing she'd decided differently? Far more often than she liked to recall.

"I imagine I'd have told her no, too," she said— and was glad she had when Chase looked grateful.

"Yeah, well, I figured that was the right way to play it," he continued. "Until about three minutes after she left, that is. Then I started worrying that I'd made a mistake. See, Graham had a quick temper, and the more I thought about that the more I wished I'd gone.

"Finally, I got in my Jeep and headed to the park. I drove around, checking the lots for their cars, but couldn't find them. Later, Rachel explained that they met at the entrance to a walking trail, and had both parked in a pull-off near it."

"So when you couldn't find them you came home?" Anne prompted after he paused a second time.

"Right. And, eventually, Rachel arrived back, so upset that I knew something was wrong the instant she walked in.

"It turned out Graham had started talking about their getting together again and she'd told him it wouldn't work. Said they simply weren't right for each other. That wasn't what he wanted to hear, though, and one thing led to another until, at some point, he shoved her.

"She said he didn't push her very hard. But they were in a wooded area and she must have slipped on some leaves or something, because she ended up on the ground. And that totally infuriated her, so she didn't say another word—just picked herself up, marched back to her car and drove home. End of story. Until yesterday morning, when we turned on the news and heard he'd been killed."

"How did she react?"

"She practically disintegrated. She'd been seeing him for months, and even though she'd decided he wasn't the love of her life, she still had feelings for him. In any event, the police were issuing their standard request for people who knew anything to contact them.''

''And she did.''

''Of course.''

''Despite her habit of avoiding difficult situations.''

''She realized there was no avoiding this one.''

That, Anne thought, was only too true. Likely, people in the park had seen Rachel and Graham together. Or, at the very least, had seen their cars parked in the same place. Which meant it would only have been a matter of time until the police learned her identity.

''So Rachel called the police,'' she said. ''And the next thing you knew those detectives were at your house.''

Chase nodded.

''And when Julie told me the 'TV people' are implying Rachel did it? Are they really?''

''Yes.''

''Do you think that's just hype, or did the detectives actually seem to suspect her?''

''Well…I'd better fill you in on some of the other details. Graham was killed with a .40-caliber Glock, which, apparently, is standard Toronto police issue. So they assume someone turned his own gun on him and—''

''He had it with him, then?''

''It seems that way. Rachel didn't see it. But he was wearing a jacket, so it could have been underneath that or in a pocket. At any rate, it wasn't found at the scene. And since it wasn't in his car or apartment, the detectives figure he was carrying it. And that the killer took it with him.''

''But if ballistics hasn't got it, there's no way of telling whether it's actually the murder weapon or not.''

''No, and…you know a lot about police procedures?''

''A fair bit.''

''Well, then, if they'd really thought it was Rachel who killed him, wouldn't they have checked her for gunpowder? Don't traces of it show up even if somebody's spent forever scrubbing their hands?''

''Uh-uh. Unless you do a gunshot residue test within a few hours, it's basically useless. They'd never have bothered with one the morning after, regardless of what they thought.''

''You're positive?''

'''Fraid so.''

Chase raked his fingers through his hair, clearly not happy with that bit of information.

''Those detectives kept coming back to one fact,'' he finally continued. ''Rachel's the last person who saw Graham alive.''

''Look,'' Anne said quietly. ''I realize how unnerving this has to be, but they're only doing their job—trying to establish exactly what happened during the time leading up to his death. And since Rachel was with him…what I'm saying is that her being with him is an entire world away from her having killed him. And they know that.''

''Right. Of course they do. But…''

''But what?''

He hesitated, then said, ''The man who phoned me. Who says he has the gun. What if he actually does, and he's figured out some way he really *can* use it to implicate her?''

Anne slowly sat back in her chair. If Rachel had absolutely nothing to do with Graham's murder, why would Chase think there was any way someone could frame her?

Because that's what his caller threatened to do, she silently answered her own question. *And even if it's not a realistic threat, it's a very frightening one.*

''Have you considered that this guy might just be some crank?'' she said. ''That he doesn't have the gun at all? Maybe he only heard about the murder on the news. And with the media insinuating that the 'girlfriend' did it, he decided to find out who Rachel was and try a shakedown.''

''Yes, I thought about that. In fact, my first assumption was that he *had* to be a nutcase. But as he kept talking, I realized he'd actually been close by while Rachel and Graham were arguing. Because he knew Graham had shoved her. Plus, he repeated a couple of things they said.

''As for the gun, I don't think there's any doubt he has it. He said Graham's initials are on the handle. Which is true. According to Rachel, some cops like to have that done, and Graham was one of them.''

Anne nodded, thinking that even if Chase's caller had the real item, they still had no way of knowing whether it was the murder weapon or not.

"Let's back up for a minute," she said. He wasn't exactly giving her the story in an orderly fashion, and unless he did she was likely to miss more information than she got.

"When you say this guy called *you,* you mean that you answered the phone and he didn't ask for Rachel? He just went ahead and laid his story on you?"

"No, I mean he specifically called *me.* I've got a separate line in my office and that's the one he used, not the house number."

"And what about his voice? I don't suppose it sounded even slightly familiar?"

"No. Actually, it barely sounded real. It had a strange, metallic tone."

"As if he was using some sort of electronic device?"

"Exactly. So even if he was someone I know, I wouldn't have realized it. But the immediate question's not, who is he? It's, what do I do about him? Because he said he'd call back in a couple of days. And if I don't have the money for him, he's going to plant the gun someplace that will incriminate Rachel."

Fleetingly, Anne wondered what sort of place he had in mind, then told herself that wasn't important and said, "Chase, a lowlife can make any threats he wants. But as long as her fingerprints aren't on the gun it can't incriminate her."

"That's exactly what I told him."

"And he said?"

"He...said they *are* on it."

"Oh?"

The word came out far less casually than she'd intended, but Chase barely seemed to notice. He just gave her a shrug, then elaborated.

"His version of what happened wasn't quite the same as Rachel's. According to him, after Graham pushed her he pulled his gun. She got up and made a grab for it. And while they both had hold of it, it went off. Graham was shot and she ran—leaving the gun lying on the ground. Which is how this jerk claims he ended up with it."

"Ah." When no subtle way of wording her next question came to her, Anne simply said, "You're sure things couldn't have played out that way? That the gun didn't accidentally go off, and Rachel's just too frightened to admit—"

"No. After Graham pushed her, she got up and left. Period. She'd never lie to me about something that important. Whereas this guy wants money from me, so he had to concoct a story he could threaten to tell the police."

"But...Chase, I know I'm repeating myself, but his claiming Rachel's fingerprints are on the gun doesn't make it true. And as long as they really aren't—"

"That's what we kept telling ourselves last night. Then we realized it might not matter. I mean, what if nobody's prints are on it by this point? What if he's wiped it clean? And then he *does* plant it? Wouldn't those detectives figure Rachel was the one who'd wiped off the prints? Because some of them were hers?"

"Not if you tell them about this guy. Not if they're expecting the gun to turn up someplace that—"

"There's more," Chase interrupted.

She looked at him, certain that whatever the "more" was, it wasn't good.

"He didn't only talk about planting the gun. He said he'd know, right away, if I told the cops he'd called me. And that if I did, it would be game over. That he had a whole bag of tricks up his sleeve."

"Chase, regardless of what threats he made it still doesn't mean—"

"I know. Rationally, both Rachel and I are aware that what you're saying is right."

"Then…I guess that gets me back to the question of why you didn't contact the police."

He wearily shook his head. "Because when I told her about the call she went into total panic. And by the time we'd finished discussing things I wasn't sure what the hell to do. We…would you like to hear where we ended up?"

"Yes, of course."

"Well, the longer we thought about it, the more logical it seemed that this guy's the real killer. Our best scenario was that he went to the park looking for someone to mug and just happened to come across Rachel and Graham.

"Then, after Rachel left, he decided Graham

would make as good a victim as anyone. But instead of cooperating, Graham pulled his gun. And that's where the story came from about a struggle and the gun going off and…what do you think?''

"I…it's certainly possible."

Rapidly, Anne began evaluating just *how* possible that scenario might be. Assuming Rachel's version of events was accurate, a mugger theory held water. And, one way or another, the killer could have learned her identity. But beyond what had happened while Rachel was with Graham, they were into pure speculation.

Looking at Chase again, she said, "*Was* Graham robbed? Was his wallet missing when his body was discovered?''

"I don't know. The detectives didn't say anything about that, and we've heard nothing on the news. But if it *was,* then the rest falls neatly into place, doesn't it? We've got some creep lurking in the park, with robbery on his mind, who kills Graham. Then he has the idea of going after *serious* money with a little extortion.

"And now, assuming he actually *can* make Rachel appear guilty, that's exactly what he'll do if I cross him up. Because if the cops charged her they sure wouldn't be looking for *him.* So…well, we just didn't want to call them and come to regret it.''

Pushing her hair back from her face, Anne tried to consider a hundred different things at once.

"So? What do you think?" Chase asked again.

She hesitated, then said, "You might hate me for

this, but I still think you should have talked to the police last night.''

"I just didn't feel I could," he said, shaking his head. "Aside from anything else, I wasn't sure they'd believe me."

"Why not?"

"Well, we got to thinking they might figure I'd only made up the extortionist story—as a way of throwing suspicion off Rachel.

"Don't look so skeptical," he added before Anne even realized she was. "When the detectives interviewed her, they asked if she'd seen anyone near the clearing. And she said she hadn't. So for me to tell them there *was* someone there, and that he'd phoned me with his threat..."

"Chase, Rachel and Graham were having a heated argument. It's hardly going to surprise the cops if she didn't notice someone hiding in the trees."

"Even so...well, at this point it doesn't matter. It turns out I've got a witness to the guy's call. Julie overheard me talking to him. But she didn't tell me she had until after she came over here this morning.

"And, last night, Rachel...I guess what really had her so terrified was not knowing exactly how much this guy might be capable of, or what he had in mind when he talked about having a whole bag of tricks up his sleeve."

"That's what intimidation's all about," Anne said gently.

"I know. I just hadn't realized how effective it can be."

She let the silence grow for a few moments, then said, "You could still call the police now."

Chase didn't reply, just stared silently across the pool. Finally, he turned and caught her gaze.

He was clearly both exhausted and troubled, the picture of a man who'd lain awake all night, wrestling with a problem far greater than his coping ability.

She felt badly for him and wished she could do a lot more to help than merely pressing him to call the police.

"What if I phone them and it makes things worse for Rachel?" he said at last. "Even after I explain everything, won't they suspect I had some other reason for waiting so long? Wonder if she actually does have something to hide? Figure we might have spent last night and this morning trying to decide if we'd be better off keeping quiet?"

Anne didn't reply, but he was raising a valid concern. It lessened her certainty that calling the cops was the right way to go.

"Hell, maybe they'd even wonder if Julie really did overhear that call," he was saying. "They might suspect we just told her we needed her help, and coached her about what to say."

He looked out over the pool once more, then said, "But you're really convinced I should phone them?"

"Give me a minute to think," she murmured. A whole lot of questions were drifting in the slipstreams of her mind. One of them, though, overshadowed all the others combined.

How likely was it that Rachel actually *had* killed Graham Lowe?

CHASE SAT WATCHING ANNE and wishing he could read minds. He didn't want to interrupt her thoughts, but he was awfully curious about exactly what they were. Awfully curious and awfully worried. Her reaction would be probably much like a jury's, so...

He stopped himself right there. His sister was innocent, which made thinking along those lines absolutely ridiculous. Still, he had the distinct impression that Anne didn't entirely believe Rachel's story.

Not that she seemed anywhere near as suspicious as those detectives had been. On the other hand, she didn't know all the details yet.

Maybe, before he got into the rest of them, he should explain that Rachel could never in a million years kill a mouse, let alone a man. Tell her, for example, about the time he'd bought a wasp trap for the backyard—and how she'd refused to let him put it up, even though eating outside meant either having to share your food with the damned wasps or risk getting stung.

Finally, he decided that, for the moment, he'd be wise to just keep quiet and see what Anne had to say.

Looking away from her, he ordered himself to think about *anything* other than Rachel's problem. He'd been dwelling on it, nonstop, since yesterday morning. If he didn't start taking the occasional mental break he'd be a basket case in no time.

After rejecting a couple of possible subjects for thought, he settled on the question of why a woman like Anne was unattached. She was great looking, obviously smart, and she had both a friendly manner and a smile that made him feel warm inside whenever she flashed it at him. So why wasn't there a husband on the scene? Or a boyfriend?

Actually, he knew why there was no husband. She was divorced. Rachel had learned that from the real estate woman—via their ex-neighbor. As for lack of a boyfriend, he was only guessing at that.

If there was one, though, surely he'd be here helping her settle in. Or she'd have said she had someone coming later to help her arrange the furniture. When women were unavailable, or not interested, they always let men know.

But why on earth had he started contemplating the status of Anne Barrett's love life? He certainly had no ideas about …

No, *definitely* no ideas along those lines. Not with her or any other woman. Julie, Rachel and he might not add up to a standard household, but their living arrangement worked for all three of them. And…

Rachel. Despite his best efforts, his thoughts returned to the problem at hand. The serious, ugly problem.

He looked across the patio table at Anne again, deciding he *would* have a shot at telling her what kind of person his sister was. But before he could begin, the gate between the yards creaked. When he glanced over, Rachel was standing in the opening.

"Mind if I join the party?" she asked tentatively. "Julie's gone next door to play with Becky for a while. But before she left, she told me what you were talking about."

"My sister," he said to Anne, even though she'd already have figured that out.

She smiled across the yard at Rachel, which, for some reason, made him feel a touch better about this damn situation.

"I'm Anne Barrett," she was saying. "And you're exactly what the party needs."

While Rachel Nicholson started around the end of the pool, Anne tried to size her up without being totally transparent about it.

Six or seven years younger than her brother, somewhere in her mid-twenties, she had deep brown eyes the same rich chocolate shade as Chase's. At the moment, there were dark shadows beneath them. That, along with her bleak expression, gave her an utterly stressed-out appearance.

At about Anne's height, five foot five or six, and as slightly built, she certainly didn't look like a woman who could wrestle control of a gun from a police detective. Of course, Chase's caller hadn't said she'd gotten control of it—only that it had gone off while she'd been trying to.

As Rachel neared the patio, Anne said, "I hope you don't think I'm sticking my nose in where it doesn't belong, but—"

"Oh, no, that's not what I think at all. Julie explained that she came over because she figured you might be able to help. And if Chase thinks so, too…''

After shooting her brother an anxious glance, Rachel looked at Anne again. ''I'll really appreciate any advice you can give us. Chase and I were even wondering whether we should talk to a lawyer, but I guess he's mentioned that.''

''I hadn't quite gotten to it,'' he told her.

''We were still trying to decide what you should do about the extortion call,'' Anne said.

Not that it was actually a matter of deciding. Rather, it was a matter of convincing them to report it. All taking time to think had done was reassure her that was the only thing to do.

Of course, those detectives *would* wonder why Chase hadn't phoned them last night. He was right about that. Still, he had to call them.

''Didn't Chase tell you we'd already decided?'' Rachel was saying uneasily. ''We're going to keep quiet about it.''

''Well…I understand why that seems like a reasonable idea, but—''

''Anne, the guy said he'd know if Chase talked to the police and—''

''Yes, I realize that's what he said, but it's awfully unlikely. How would he find out?''

''I think he's a cop.''

The way Rachel said that, with conviction and not a second's hesitation, told Anne she hadn't arrived at the conclusion on the spur of the moment.

''There are all kinds of dirty cops,'' she continued.

''I probably sound paranoid, but I went with Graham for almost six months and I learned an awful lot about them.''

''I don't think you sound paranoid,'' Anne said honestly. ''I was a P.I. for long enough to learn a lot about them, too.''

Rachel nodded, looking relieved. ''Then you know the kind of scams they've got going. Now and then, Graham would tell me about some of them. And about how, if a cop has the right connections, he can find out pretty much whatever he wants. So when this guy says he'll learn if Chase tells those detectives about the call, then I have to think that maybe he will.''

''I guess it's possible.''

Anne hesitated, but she didn't want Rachel thinking that by ''possible'' she meant ''likely,'' so she added, ''The thing is, I have a problem with the idea of this guy in the park being a cop. Mugging just isn't the sort of thing dirty cops are normally into.''

''But that doesn't mean one of them can't be. Or there could be more than one person involved. What if the mugger wasn't a cop, but the guy who phoned Chase was? Maybe the mugger told him what had happened and the cop came up with the extortion plan.''

''No,'' Anne said. ''A mugging goes wrong and turns into a killing, then the killer admits this to a cop? That just doesn't add up.''

''But…it might. If we're talking about a crooked cop and a criminal who've worked together before.

And maybe it was the mugger who came up with the extortion idea, but he realized he'd have a better chance of pulling it off if he had help. So he told the cop exactly what happened, then they came up with their plan to…'' As her words trailed off, Rachel shook her head.

"Look," she continued a moment later, "I know that doesn't really add up, either. But when someone says that if Chase talks to the police about the phone call I'll find myself framed for murder, it scares the hell out of me.''

"Well, that's hardly surprising," Anne told her. "And who knows? Maybe a cop *is* somehow involved.''

It must have been apparent that she was only trying to humor Rachel, because Chase said, "Rachel's intuition is surprisingly good.''

"Okay," she said slowly. "Then let's assume there *is* a cop. Let's even assume he *could* find out if Chase contacts those detectives.''

Rachel nodded for her to go on.

"After Chase has told them what the guy threatened to do, they'd hardly be surprised if the murder weapon turned up someplace that seemed to incriminate you. Or if it had been wiped clean. And they—''

"They might not be surprised," Rachel interrupted, her voice quavering a little. "But it would give them one more piece of evidence against me. And even though everything they've got is circumstantial, if they end up with enough…''

"Everything?" Anne glanced at Chase, wondering what—and how much—he hadn't told her.

"We didn't really get beyond talking about the phone call," he was saying to his sister. "That and what happened in the park. She doesn't know about your clothes—yet."

CHAPTER THREE

WHILE ANNE WAITED TO HEAR about Rachel's "clothes," Rachel sat looking as if that was the last topic in the world she wanted to discuss.

Finally, she said, "When Graham and I were arguing... Chase told you the details about that?"

"Everything you told me," he said before Anne could reply.

"Well...my shorts got torn when I fell, and my top ended up with a grass stain on it. So I just pitched them in the garbage after I came home—didn't even bother trying to get the stain out.

"Maybe that sounds like an overreaction," she quickly added, "but I was really upset. And I knew that every time I looked at those clothes they'd remind me of how badly we'd ended things. Of course, I had no idea that Graham... So it just didn't occur to me that anyone would care about what I'd had on. Not until those detectives asked.

"They said it was strictly routine, that they just wanted to have a look to verify my statement. But as soon as I started explaining that I'd thrown the things away, I knew they were thinking there'd been bloodstains on them. That...I killed Graham."

"You mean your clothes weren't still in the

trash?'' Anne said. ''You couldn't have dug them out and—''

''The garbage gets collected first thing Thursday mornings,'' Chase told her. ''It was picked up long before they arrived.''

''I see.'' The more of this story she heard, the better she understood why the police would consider his sister a serious suspect.

''They wanted to look at the underwear I'd been wearing, too,'' Rachel murmured. ''They said that maybe there'd be a grass stain where my shorts tore or something.'' She shook her head. ''They might as well have just said that maybe some blood spatters had soaked through.''

''But at least you still had the underwear to show them, didn't you?''

''Yes, only I'd washed it. I put a load in the machine before I went to bed on Wednesday. They were suspicious about that, too.''

Hardly surprising. Rachel seemed like an intelligent-enough woman that—if even a speck of Graham's blood had gotten on her—she'd have disposed of every stitch she'd had on. And, for all the detectives knew, she could have shown them *any* underwear fresh from the wash.

But if she was guilty, if her clothes had actually been evidence that she'd killed Graham, why admit to throwing them out?

She'd have realized that would make the police suspicious. So why wouldn't she have done the obvious? Produced clothes that looked similar to what she'd been wearing? Eyewitnesses were notoriously inaccurate, which meant that even if people had seen her in the park…

Chase had been home when she left, though. If she'd tried lying, he'd have known.

Anne glanced at him, remembering he'd also been there waiting when Rachel returned. If she'd arrived back with blood on her clothes, he could hardly have helped noticing. Which meant her story had to be true—unless there'd been only a few, inconspicuous, traces of blood. Or unless Chase was trying to help her cover up what she'd done.

That thought had barely formed before it was joined by another, even more disquieting, one. What if Chase had played a role in Graham's death?

She licked her suddenly dry lips and surreptitiously looked at him again. She could almost feel his distress, but was he *just* worried about Rachel? Or was he afraid those detectives figured he might have been involved in the shooting?

He'd admitted going to the park. And she only had his say-so that he hadn't found Rachel and Graham there. What if he actually had? While they'd been in the midst of their argument? Or maybe after Graham had pushed her down?

Of course, every one of those questions, and then some, would have occurred to the cops. They'd have suspected that Chase might have done a lot more than simply drive around—which was undoubtedly the *real* reason they'd questioned him at length.

Lord, for all she knew, she was sitting here with

not one but two people who were at risk of being charged with murder.

Despite the warmth of the sun, she suddenly felt chilled. She'd barely met Chase and Rachel, knew virtually nothing about either of them. What if they were both lying to her?

She had to figure out whether they were, and to do that she needed more information, so she said to Rachel, "Why don't you go over what else the detectives asked about. Aside from your clothes. Start at the beginning and try to remember everything."

"Well…they wanted to know about my relationship with Graham. How long we'd been seeing each other and why we broke up. Then they had me go over what happened on Wednesday. Minute by minute, from the time I met him until I got back to my car."

"All right, let's hear what you told them."

Rachel leaned forward, resting her elbows on the table, and began.

Her account proved to be a fill-in-the-blanks elaboration of Chase's. Graham had wanted them to get back together. She'd said it wouldn't work. That led to their argument, his shoving her and her leaving.

"The detectives already knew I'd fallen," she continued. "At least they knew someone had. The crime-scene team established that the leaves had been disturbed not far from his body."

She took a deep breath, then added, "That means he was killed right in the clearing where I left him.

And every time I think about that I wonder whether he'd still be alive if I hadn't just walked away.''

''Don't do that to yourself,'' Chase said quietly. ''You had no way of knowing anything would happen.''

When Anne glanced at him, his dark eyes were filled with concern. It seemed genuine enough to make her almost certain that he knew nothing about what had happened in the park except what his sister had told him.

But her father's voice was whispering in her ear, saying, *Never trust a brown-eyed man, darling.*

It was one of the bits of advice he'd been giving her since he'd first realized she was noticing boys— always delivering the line straight-faced, waiting a beat, then adding, *And never trust a blue-eyed one, either.*

Turning her mind back to the moment, she focused on Rachel again. ''If Graham was killed right in that clearing,'' she said, mentally sorting through her thoughts as she spoke, ''it couldn't have happened long after you left. He wouldn't have just stayed standing where he was indefinitely.''

''It was after I got back to my car and drove off, though. Because I didn't hear the shot.''

''A few people in the park did,'' Chase interjected.

''And none of them investigated?''

''No. According to the news, they all assumed it was a car backfiring. Maybe, if there'd been more than one...''

''Maybe,'' she agreed, still wondering exactly

what the truth was. "How long did it take to walk back to your car?" she asked Rachel.

"Only three or four minutes."

That added up. Someone lurking in the trees wouldn't have stepped out the moment she left the clearing. He'd have held off for a bit, in case she decided to come back, before confronting Graham.

Then the encounter between the two men would have taken a little time. So Rachel could easily have been gone before... The question was, had she been?

"After you finished telling the detectives what happened in the park," she said, "where did the interview go from there?"

Rachel's eyes filled with tears. "They touched on a couple of other things, then they came right out and asked if I'd killed Graham."

The air turned deathly still. Even the aspens ceased their rustling, as if breathlessly waiting for the tale to continue.

Anne waited, as well. Then, when the silence grew uncomfortable, she said, "You know, asking if you killed him and actually believing you did are two different things. People almost never answer yes to a question like that, even if they're guilty. But the police always ask. To see what reaction they get. Sometimes, it tells them a lot."

"My reaction was that I started to cry," Rachel murmured. "I knew there was no way Graham and I should get back together, but I was still a little in love with him. And even though I was awfully angry the other night..." She paused to wipe away a few tears that were making good their escape, then shook her head as more began to flow.

Her distress reminded Anne what she'd liked least about being a private investigator—having to press people who were so emotionally fragile they shouldn't be forced to answer questions.

And when it came to Rachel, not only was she upset about Graham's murder, she knew she was a suspect. That would be more than enough to induce emotional fragility. Regardless of whether she was innocent or guilty.

PEERING THROUGH A CRACK in the gate, Julie watched Rachel cry and tried to keep from crying herself. It was hard to do, now that she knew things were even worse than she'd realized.

When she'd asked Daddy if the police thought Rachel had killed Graham, he'd tried to make it sound as if they didn't. Not *really*, at least. But they must. 'Cuz a minute ago, just as she was reaching for the latch, she'd heard Rachel say the detectives came right out and asked her if she'd done it.

After hearing that, Julie just hadn't been able to open the gate until she'd heard a little more. Then Anne had started saying that maybe the police asking wasn't as bad as it seemed. And that hadn't been a good time to interrupt, 'cuz she'd wanted to hear *why* Anne thought it wasn't so bad.

But after Anne was finished, Rachel had started crying, and she never liked anyone to see her cry, 'specially Julie, so—

Her thoughts stopped dead as a wasp zoomed past her nose and began to hover midair, directly above the plate she was carrying. Rats! She should have put plastic wrap on it.

Slowly, she took a step backward. The wasp stayed right with her, only an inch above the sandwiches.

Okay, what should she do? If she stepped forward again and reached for the latch, she might get stung. But if she didn't, the wasp was going to land. And she could never, ever, not in a zillion years, eat food a wasp had walked on.

Deciding, she called, "Dad? Dad, come open the gate. Fast! But be careful 'cuz there's a wasp."

A chair scraped across Anne's patio; a second later she could see her father heading for the fence.

"Careful," she said again, as he neared it.

He cautiously opened the gate, then slowly brushed at the air in front of the wasp. It was a trick she'd never dare try, but it sometimes made them back off. When it did this time, she stopped holding her breath.

"I came home from Becky's 'cuz it was getting near lunchtime," she explained as he took the plate from her. "But when I looked out from the kitchen you were all sitting there talking. So I made sandwiches and was gonna call you. Then I thought that maybe Anne didn't have any food in her house, so I made an extra one. That was okay, huh?"

"Of course," he said as they started toward the

patio. "It was very thoughtful. Hope you like peanut butter and jelly," he added to Anne.

"One of my favorites."

"It's grape jelly," Julie told her, pretending not to notice the way Rachel was wiping her eyes. "And crunchy peanut butter."

"Mmm. That's the best combination going." Anne gave her a friendly smile, then pushed back her chair and said, "I'll go get us something to drink."

"Can I help?"

"Sure. You'll know what everyone would like. Not that I have much to choose from yet, but..." She shrugged and smiled again, then turned toward the house.

Julie followed along inside, not letting herself look back at Rachel.

"A mess, isn't it." Anne gestured toward a stack of cartons.

"Kind of. But that's okay when you just moved in."

"I guess. Orange juice, iced tea or water," she added, checking the fridge.

"Ah...juice for me. And iced tea for Dad and Rachel. Please," she added, remembering her manners.

"Coming right up." Anne took the two pitchers from the fridge and set them on the counter. "Now, if I can just find some glasses..."

"Anne?"

"Yes?" She looked up from the carton she'd stooped to open.

"You're gonna be able to help Rachel, aren't you?"

"Well, I'll do whatever I can."

"Promise?"

Anne sat back on her haunches and met Julie's gaze. "Didn't I promise earlier?"

"I thought you might have forgotten."

"No, I take promises very seriously. Rachel hasn't finished telling me the whole story, though, so I'm still not sure she really needs my help. But whether she does or not, I'll bet everything's going to be just fine."

Julie nodded, thinking "everything's going to be just fine" were the exact same words her father had used this morning. But what if both he and Anne were wrong?

That possibility made her eyes sting and her throat hurt. She didn't know what she'd do if the police put Rachel in jail.

Looking at Anne again, she reminded herself that Penelope Snow didn't really solve all the mysteries in her books. Anne did. So maybe everything *would* be fine.

"You know what?" she said.

"No, what?"

"Rachel always says that if something's scary to think about, you should just not let yourself think about it."

"You mean like noises in the night?"

Even though it wasn't exactly what she meant, she nodded.

Anne smiled. "Well, that sounds like pretty good advice to me. But here, I haven't got a clue where to find a tray, so you take a couple of these glasses, okay?"

"Sure."

She followed Anne back outside, feeling way better. For the whole rest of the day, if even one single thought about anything awful happening to Rachel snuck into her head, she was just going to chase it straight back out.

CHASE DRAINED THE LAST of his iced tea and glanced at his daughter. The sooner Rachel told Anne the rest of the details, the sooner they'd find out just how bad she thought things were. But they certainly couldn't pick up where they'd left off in front of Julie.

She popped the final bite of sandwich into her mouth, gazed longingly at the pool for a moment, then focused on Anne. "Are we still going swimming?"

"Sure. But we have to wait for a while, don't we?" she added, glancing at Chase.

He nodded. "For an hour."

"D-a-a-d, that's only when it's a big lake."

"Really? You mean they changed the rules without telling me?"

Julie grinned. "I guess."

"I don't think so," Rachel told her. "But by the time you go home and change..."

"I hear you've got a friend who lives right next door," Anne said.

"Uh-huh. My best friend. Her name's Becky."

"Well, why don't you see if she'd like a swim, too."

Way to go, Anne, Chase thought. Every minute longer that Julie was gone gave them another minute to finish talking.

"Take the plate home, hon," Rachel said as Julie pushed back her chair.

"Aren't you and Dad coming, too? Aren't you going to change?"

"Later," Chase told her.

He waited until she'd disappeared behind the gate, then looked at his sister. "Let's see how fast we can finish filling Anne in."

"You're feeling up to talking again?" she asked Rachel.

"Uh-huh, the sugar hit from that jelly helped a lot. So what else should I tell you?"

"Well…let's hear exactly what the detectives asked you about Graham's gun. Chase said they wanted to know whether he had it with him."

"Yes, and I told them I didn't think so. That if he did, I wasn't aware of it. But I'm not sure they believed me."

"Why not?"

"Because the next thing they asked was if I knew how to use it. That was just before they asked me if I'd killed him," she added, staring at a patio stone.

Anne glanced at Chase.

He nodded that she should continue. He doubted Rachel was as up to talking as she wanted them to think, but Anne couldn't help unless she had the rest of the facts.

"And *do* you know how to use a gun?" she asked quietly.

"Uh-huh. Graham taught me to shoot. He used to take me to the police target range with him."

Chase couldn't stop himself from checking Anne's reaction to that.

He'd already realized she wasn't very good at concealing her thoughts—especially considering she'd been a P.I.—and at the moment he could tell precisely what she was thinking. Learning that Rachel knew how to handle a gun would only have made those detectives more convinced she was their killer.

After a few seconds of silence, she said, "Rachel, let's talk about the would-be extortionist for a minute. You didn't even think Graham was carrying his gun, yet this guy claimed Graham drew it while you were still there, and—"

"I explained what we figure about that," Chase reminded her. "He needed a story he could threaten to tell the police, and that's what he decided on."

"There's no truth to the gun part at all," Rachel said, her voice catching a little. "Graham didn't draw his gun while I was with him, I didn't wrestle him for it and I *didn't, didn't* kill him. Anne, everything happened *exactly* the way I told you."

When she murmured "I know it did," Chase wondered if she was actually convinced. No matter how many times he assured himself that the "evidence" against his sister was entirely circumstantial, he knew how things must look to an outsider.

"Okay, then let's get back to the detectives," Anne suggested. "You told them that you simply got up and left after Graham pushed you, and what did they say?"

"Nothing."

"They just let it pass?"

Rachel nodded.

"You figure that's significant," Chase said.

"Well…yes. I've been assuming they found evidence of a struggle, been assuming that's why they figure the killer might have turned Graham's own gun on him. But if there *was* evidence, why wouldn't they have pressed Rachel about saying she just got up and walked off?"

Chase considered the question, but couldn't come up with any logical answer. "They noticed the leaves were disturbed where she fell," he finally said. "So they'd hardly have missed something more obvious."

He hesitated then, afraid of jumping to a conclusion just because he wanted it to be true. But since it struck him as the only possible one, he added, "Which means there can't have been any struggle. And *that* means," he continued, looking at Rachel with a sudden sense of euphoria, "we don't have to worry about our extortionist. Because if he tells the cops you wrestled with Graham for his gun, they'll know he's lying."

"Chase?" Anne said.

When he glanced at her, she said, "*Maybe* there was no evidence of a struggle. But maybe there was, and the detectives just had some reason for not asking Rachel about it."

A reason like wanting to give her enough rope to hang herself? he thought, the euphoria gone as quickly as it had come.

"What sort of reason?" Rachel asked.

"Nothing really comes to mind," Anne told her. "So Chase was probably right—there likely wasn't any sign of a struggle. But if there wasn't, why would the cops think Graham might have been shot with his own gun?"

"Because he was killed with a Glock?" Chase said.

"Well…I guess that could be it, although the police are hardly the only people who have Glocks. But let's get back to why they didn't ask about a struggle.

"If we assume it was because there *wasn't* one, we get an entirely different scenario of what happened in the clearing. In it, the killer would have stepped out of the woods with a gun aimed at Graham, and—"

"No, that doesn't make sense," Rachel said. "Because Graham wasn't stupid. If someone was pointing a gun at him, he'd have simply handed over his wallet. And if he had, why would the guy have killed him?"

When Anne was silent again, Chase's throat went dry. They were close to something important. He felt certain they were. So why didn't she know what it was?

As the seconds slowly passed, he told himself she was merely taking time to think. Finally, he couldn't stop himself from asking what she was thinking *about*.

"Just something my father used to tell me," she said. "Do you know he's a private investigator?"

"Yes, Julie mentioned it. She said you used to work for him. But what did he tell you?"

"That I should always guard against tunnel vision, never lock into only one explanation when there might be others. So I was remembering that—and trying to figure out what others there could be when it comes to Graham's murder."

Chase retreated into wait mode once more, simply watching Anne until the silence grew too much for him again.

"And?" he said when it did. "What other explanations are coming to mind?"

"Well, only one, really. That the guy in the park wasn't a mugger at all. That he followed Graham there with the specific intention of killing him."

ANNE, RACHEL AND CHASE were still talking when Julie arrived back with Becky in tow.

The two of them proceeded to be as silly as only a couple of little girls can, but even that wasn't enough to drive away the thought that had been skittering around the fringes of Anne's mind.

If no one had wrestled with Graham for his gun,

then it seemed almost inconceivable that either Rachel or Chase had any involvement in his death. Still, the fact remained that there *could* have been a struggle. And if there had been, all bets were off.

"Last one in's a rotten egg!" Becky suddenly screamed, launching herself toward the pool.

Julie cannonballed in after her and they immediately began a game of water volleyball with the beach ball they'd brought over.

"Normally, I'd tell them to keep it down," Chase said after one of them let out a piercing shriek. "But as long as they're making noise they won't be listening to us. So where were we?" he added.

"Anne was saying she wished we had more hard facts," Rachel reminded him.

"Right," she agreed, warning herself to be careful.

They'd long ago wandered away from the subject of whether the Nicholsons were going to tell the police about that extortion call, but for the past few minutes she'd been easing the conversation back toward it. And she didn't want to say anything that might make Rachel even more determined to keep it a secret.

"I'd really like to know whether Graham's wallet was taken," she continued. "Because if it was still on his body, that would definitely rule out robbery as a motive. And I'd really, really like to know whether there were signs of a struggle."

"Oh, I'd give the *world* to know that," Rachel said. "If I could just be sure it doesn't matter whether that guy tells the cops his story, if I was certain they wouldn't believe him… But is there any way we can find out?''

''Well, it's pretty tough for an outsider to get crime-scene details. I mean, you can hardly phone those detectives and start asking questions about their investigation.

''But you know, Chase,'' she added, sounding as thoughtful as she could, ''if you called them about the extortionist, then while you were talking to them you might be able to—''

''No,'' Rachel said firmly.

CHAPTER FOUR

ANNE TURNED TO CHASE, thinking that surely, regardless of his sister's fears, he must realize the only rational way to deal with extortion threats was by reporting them.

However, it was Rachel who spoke. "We talked this into the ground last night," she said. "And telling those detectives will only make things worse."

Anne focused on her once more. "Rachel...listen to me, okay? If you keep quiet about this guy you're putting them at a major disadvantage. And you're not helping your own situation, either.

"They're making a whole lot of false assumptions because they aren't aware someone was in the park watching you. Someone who may have been following Graham, waiting for a chance to kill him. But if Chase told them—"

"If he did, they probably wouldn't believe him."

"You know, at this point I'm so into overload I can't even remember why you figure that."

"Because the guy called me at dinnertime yesterday," Chase said. "By now, I'd be telling the cops about it almost twenty-four hours later. So, obviously, they'd suspect it was just a story we came up with to throw their suspicions off Rachel."

"But I really don't think—"

"Anne?" Rachel said. "Aside from what the police would figure, if the guy really has some way of finding out if Chase calls them—"

"We don't know he does."

"But we don't know he *doesn't!* What if he does? Then he follows through on his threat, and it turns out there *were* signs of a struggle? Those detectives would be *certain* I'm guilty."

"But—"

"Look, as I said before, I learned a lot about cops from Graham. And maybe your father used to warn you about tunnel vision, but I doubt either Westin or Providence has the slightest concern about it."

"Those are the detectives who came to the house," Chase explained.

"All they're thinking," Rachel continued, "is that I was with Graham the evening he was killed and that I was furious with him. Plus, they're convinced he was carrying his gun. A gun I knew how to use. To their minds, that gives me motive, means and opportunity.

"Then we've got those damned clothes I threw out. All I need is one more strike against me, whether it's real or trumped up, and I'll find myself sitting in a jail cell facing murder charges."

Taking a long, slow breath, Anne told herself to remain cool and logical. "Rachel," she said at last, "there's no way in the world anyone would charge you with murder. Even if those detectives *do* think you killed Graham—"

"What?" she interrupted, her eyes luminous with tears. "Are you going to say they'd only charge me with manslaughter? Because I killed him in the heat of passion? Or maybe even involuntary manslaughter? Because I was only trying to take the gun away from him when it went off?

"Anne, I didn't have a thing to do with Graham's death! And I don't want to go through the rest of my life with people thinking that I must have because I was charged with...with *anything!*

"And what if it got to trial and I was headline news? Then I'd *always* be a killer in people's eyes, even if I wasn't convicted. My life would be ruined when I've done nothing at all.

"So maybe this guy who phoned would know if Chase told the cops about his call and maybe he wouldn't. But I'm not taking the chance he would."

Anne looked at Chase again. "Is that the way you feel, too?"

He shook his head. "How I feel doesn't matter. I promised Rachel the final decision was hers. After all, she's the one at risk, the one who could end up sitting in that jail cell. Not me."

"I see," she murmured.

"Anne?" Rachel said.

"Yes?"

"I've told you about all I can, and...as much as I care about whatever else you've got to say, I'm getting a migraine. I thought I'd headed it off this morning, but it's coming back. So unless there's anything more you desperately still need to ask me, maybe you and Chase can…''

"We know where to find you if we can't," he told her.

She pushed back her chair. "I realize how pig-headed you figure I'm being about that call," she added to Anne. "But…''

"I understand." She might not think they were handling this the right way, but she *did* understand.

"Good. Well…it doesn't seem like nearly enough to just say thanks. But I'm really, really grateful that you're trying to help. And whatever—''

"Rachel?" Julie called from the pool. "Are you going home to put on your bathing suit?''

"No, hon, I'm getting migraine flashes, so I'm going to take something and lie down. Maybe I'll come back over later," she added, starting for the gate.

Anne watched Rachel skirt the end of the pool, mentally replaying her explanation of why she didn't want Chase to tell the cops about that call.

Everything she'd said had referred to *her*—how the police might charge *her,* how *her* life could be affected. She hadn't uttered a single word about the possibility that they suspected Chase, as well.

And he'd said nothing to that effect, either. Rachel's the one at risk, he'd said. Not me.

So, regardless of how much time those detectives spent questioning him yesterday, and despite knowing he'd gone after his sister, they'd left both Nicholsons with the same message: Rachel was a suspect; Chase wasn't.

Anne considered that, wondering whether some neighbor had seen him arriving home from the park.

Since people had heard the gunshot, the cops would have an accurate fix on the time. And, quite possibly, they'd ruled out Chase because he'd been back before Graham was killed.

Whatever the reason, though, it seemed obvious they didn't suspect him.

She was glad of that, but she couldn't stop wishing they didn't suspect his sister, either. Or, more accurately, she wished there wasn't so much evidence pointing toward Rachel's guilt. Because the way things stood, she might well end up being charged. And now that they'd spent some time together, Anne had a gut feeling Rachel was innocent.

Of course, her instincts about people weren't always right. And what if she was wrong this time? Lord, she didn't even want to think about that. By saying she'd try to help before she knew the facts, she'd gotten herself into something worse than she'd expected and in far deeper than she wanted to be.

But while common sense was telling her it was time to back off, what sort of relationship would she have with her new neighbors if she said, "Well, this is as far as I go. See you around"? Not a good one, that was for sure.

Glancing at Chase, she silently admitted there was another reason she didn't want to back off.

She rarely met a man who interested her. Yet the very first moment she'd seen *this* man she'd felt a tug of attraction. And getting to know him a little had told her he might be someone she could really come to like.

Actually, to be deep-down honest, she already really liked him. So she hardly wanted to say she'd decided that trying to help his sister was a bad idea.

But what would happen if her ''helping'' turned up even more evidence of Rachel's guilt?

The answer was obvious. Rachel would be in jail. And how would Chase feel about someone who'd had a hand in putting her behind bars?

Ordering herself not to go there, Anne forced her mind off the personal aspect of this and back to the broader picture.

''Let me ask you something,'' she said to Chase. ''If you aren't going to report your extortionist to the police, what do you intend to do about him?''

CHASE SAT STARING at his daughter, willing her to pick this instant to climb out of the pool and come over to the patio. If he could just manage that minor bit of mental telepathy he wouldn't have to answer Anne's question—which he definitely didn't want to do.

He had no idea how he was going to deal with the extortionist. Hell, he hadn't even given much thought to what his alternatives were. And if he had to admit that to Anne she'd figure he was an utter moron.

But ever since he'd turned on the news yesterday morning, there'd been so much to worry about that he'd simply penciled the extortion threat in toward the bottom of his list.

After all, the guy had said he'd get back to him in "a couple of days." And with this being Friday, a couple of days probably meant Monday. Whereas those detectives breathing down Rachel's neck seemed like a much more immediate threat.

"Can I assume you aren't going to give him the two hundred thousand?" Anne said.

Damn. His attempt at telepathy had failed. Neither Julie nor Becky had even glanced in his direction.

Resigning himself to his fate, he looked across the table. "I don't have two hundred thousand dollars. I don't have anything close to that."

"Could you come up with it? If you wanted to?"

As she was speaking, a thought struck him. Even if he *could,* surely no bank would hand him that much money in cash. And cash was what his caller wanted.

After he'd said as much to Anne, she slowly shook her head. "I'm not certain what that tells us. It might mean he doesn't know much about how banks work, so he doesn't realize it could be a stumbling block. On the other hand, he might be sophisticated enough to know there'd be ways of arranging it."

"You really think there would?"

She nodded. "The bank wouldn't be happy about it. And they'd probably want you to be accompanied by an armed guard, or sign some sort of release. Still, if it was *your* money, and you insisted on cash... You haven't answered my question, though. *Could* you come up with that much?"

When he eyed her uncertainly, she said, "I'm not

trying to pry into your personal finances, but *could* you?''

''Well…probably. I've got a good relationship with the manager at my trust company. But you're not suggesting I pay this jerk, are you?'' He couldn't imagine that was what she had in mind, yet he didn't know what else she'd be getting at.

''No, of course not. If you did he'd be on your back forever. It's just that…''

Looking lost in thought, she absently pushed her hair back off her cheek. And as crazy as it seemed, given that they were in the midst of this conversation, he suddenly found himself thinking she was an incredibly sexy woman.

Not that he hadn't realized it before. Even though his mind had been pretty much occupied with other things from the moment they'd met, he'd certainly noticed she was a terrific-looking woman.

But just a moment ago, something about the fluid motion of her hand, about the way her dark hair danced with auburn highlights as it moved in the sunshine, had gone straight to his groin. And started him imagining her brushing *his* hair away from *his* face. As a prelude to a kiss.

He swallowed hard, unable to force his gaze from the lushness of her lips. Then he saw that she was watching him watch her and he felt hot all over.

Scrambling for something—anything—to say, he settled on, ''You know what I think Rachel's biggest fear is? That those detectives are so convinced she killed Graham they won't be trying to learn who the *real* killer is.''

Anne nodded, allowing him to relax a little. She was going to pretend she hadn't noticed him leering at her like a sex-crazed adolescent.

"Unfortunately, it's a valid fear," she said. "Once cops decide a suspect's guilty, they put all their energy into looking for evidence to support that conclusion. But if they're wrong, no one's out there trying to learn who really committed the crime.''

"Then maybe *that's* what I should be doing about my extortionist," he said.

When she looked as if she wasn't sure what he meant, he added, "Since we figure *he's* probably the real killer, maybe I should be trying to learn who he is.''

She gave him a small smile; it make his pulse race.

"Have you ever considered being a detective?'' she asked.

"You mean that's what I *should* be doing?''

"I mean you've got the right instincts. I've been sitting here thinking that if the police are as focused on Rachel as it sounds, then unless *somebody* figures out who really killed Graham…''

"She could be in as much trouble as she's afraid she is," Chase concluded.

"Exactly. And that's why I was asking if you could come up with the money. Because whether you can or not might be significant—in figuring out who killed him, I mean.''

"Go on," he said, leaning forward in his chair.

"You said this guy phoned on your office line."

He nodded.

"So he specifically wanted to talk to you. To demand money from *you,* not from Rachel."

"That would be because she doesn't have any. She's a freelance photographer, and it's sometimes a while between assignments."

"Yes, but how did your guy *know* he'd be smarter to try hitting on you? Or that you might be able to come up with such a large amount?

"For that matter, how did he know she had a brother? And that the two of you are close?"

"I have no idea," Chase said slowly. The questions had never even occurred to him. "I guess he did his homework."

"Maybe. But he'd have had to do a lot of it fast. Just think about the timing. Graham's body wasn't discovered until yesterday morning. The media were only referring to Rachel as Graham's girlfriend. And the police would never have released her name to any nosy Joe Public. But by dinnertime he not only knew who she was, he knew she had a brother who'd be a better bet for coming up with money than she was."

"And from that you're concluding…?"

"Well, 'concluding' is a little strong, but I'm thinking he might be someone Rachel knows. Or at least someone who knew Graham and knew who his girlfriend was."

Chase could feel his adrenaline starting to pump. He hadn't been *seriously* imagining he could figure out who his caller was, yet if Anne was right they actually might be able to do it. "You think he's *likely* someone Rachel knows?"

"I…yes. He could have found out about her just by asking around, but the obvious people to talk to would have been Graham's friends. And if Graham was like most cops, they'd all have been cops, too— people who'd be suspicious of someone who seemed curious about him right after he'd been murdered. So it's far more likely he already knew who Rachel was."

Anne's words triggered a thought.

"What about her dirty-cop theory? Aside from Graham's friends, since he used to take her to the shooting range, a lot of cops would have met her there."

She nodded. "So if there actually *are* two people working together, maybe she was guessing right. One of them killed Graham and the other had the information they needed to try blackmailing you.

"On the other hand, there's nothing to say a crooked cop can't be both the murderer *and* have access to information about the case. Which would get us back to a single person."

Chase rubbed his jaw, thinking that there was a hell of a lot more linking things together in this detecting business than he'd realized. And Anne seemed damn good. So good he could almost believe that, with her help—

"Dad?" Julie called.

As he turned toward the pool, she said, "Aren't

you and Anne *ever* coming in? Becky and I are gonna be wrinkled as prunes soon.''

"Well, you could always come out for a while."

Both girls gave him a horrified look, shouted "No way!" then sank beneath the surface.

"I'm *still* wishing we had more information," Anne said when he turned his attention back to her. "I mean, we can make a nice argument for the killer having known Graham, but it's still only speculation. Whereas if I was *certain* we could rule out robbery as a motive, I'd be *almost* certain the murder wasn't a random killing. That the killer had a motive. And if we knew who might have wanted him dead…"

"Maybe Rachel would have an idea about that. And no matter how bad her migraine is, if we tell her we have to talk to her, she'll talk."

"Give me a minute to think," Anne murmured. She wasn't sure how far she was prepared to go with this and she had to decide.

Trying to ID a murderer was a giant leap beyond simply listening and offering her opinion. And if she made that leap, Chase would expect to be right there beside her.

He'd never go for the idea of her getting actively involved on her own. Convincing him he shouldn't be part of things would be impossible.

She glanced at him, thinking he seemed like a man who could take care of himself. Which meant that having him around wouldn't be totally negative.

Still, on the down side, he was a rank amateur when it came to this sort of situation. So knowing that he'd insist was another reason for her to stop before she really got started.

Besides, there was still the possibility that Rachel had actually killed Graham. And that made the prospect of going even an inch further very, very unnerving.

Making her decision, she said, "What you need is a professional investigator." Then she bit her tongue, because the offer to do more than just give that advice was right on the tip of it.

CHASE FELT HIS HOPEFULNESS fizzling away.

He'd been assuming that Anne and he would take things at least one step further right now and talk to Rachel some more. Because considering the way the police were homing in on her with their tunnel vision, and the extortionist's promise to call back in a couple of days, time was of the essence.

But he could see Anne's reluctance. She'd only be going over to his place with him if he pressed, and he wasn't about to do that. He'd just be grateful for the time she'd already given them—and take her suggestion to hire someone.

"You're right," he said. "You were on such a roll I was forgetting you aren't really in the detective game anymore."

She looked decidedly relieved. "No. And I not only gave up my license but I'm badly out of practice."

He nodded, although he couldn't stop himself from

wishing she'd come out of retirement for one final case.

Thus far, she hadn't sounded out of practice to him. And he had a horrible feeling that by the time he found someone else and brought him up to speed, Rachel's fears would be reality. She'd be sitting in that jail cell.

When Anne said nothing more, he made himself ask, "Who would you recommend? Your father? Is this the sort of thing he specializes in?"

"Actually, it isn't the sort of thing any investigators specialize in. People don't often hire them to ID suspects the cops aren't even looking for.

"But my dad's one of the best in the business, so sure, I'd recommend him. The only thing is... Chase, are you absolutely determined not to tell the police about that extortion call?"

He hesitated, knowing he should, regardless of how long it was after the fact. But he'd promised Rachel. And he'd never forgive himself if he told them and it turned out to be a bad move—if the blackmailer *did* make good on his threat and it *did* put her in a worse position than she already was.

"I gave Rachel my word," he said. "So it's still her decision."

"All right," Anne said slowly. "But that means there's a problem with hiring a private detective."

"Oh?" He mentally shook his head. He'd about reached his limit as far as problems were concerned.

"In the first place, if someone calls in a lawyer or

a P.I., it fuels the cops' belief that he's guilty. Or she's guilty, in this case."

"And in the second place?" he made himself ask.

"Well, when it comes to client privilege, a private investigator doesn't get to play by lawyers' rules. He's obliged to cooperate with the police. Otherwise he risks losing his license.

"But you'd obviously want to give whoever you hired a word-by-word replay of the extortionist's call. You'd want him to know *everything,* regardless of whether it looks good or bad for Rachel. The problem would come if the cops talked to him and discovered that the two of you told him things you withheld from them."

"It would add even more fuel to the fire," he concluded.

"Precisely."

Chase said nothing more, but he caught Anne's gaze and didn't let it go.

An unsettling feeling wrapped itself around her heart. She could tell exactly what he was thinking. Since she'd given up her license, she'd be at no risk of losing it. Which meant that if *she* undertook the investigation, she wouldn't have to share anything with the cops.

That presented such a simple solution it seemed crazy to be backing off. So had she made the wrong decision? Overreacted?

After all, her only *real* concern about getting in any deeper was that Rachel might prove to be guilty. And there just couldn't be too much chance of that.

The "watcher in the woods as killer" theory seemed far more likely.

Still, was "likely" good enough that she should trust her instincts? Go with her feelings rather than her fears?

What if she did and she was wrong?

But what if she was right?

What if she was right and she tracked down the real killer? While the police were busily trying to railroad Rachel?

Suddenly, she was imagining what her father would think if that happened. He'd be so impressed...

And so *surprised,* an imaginary voice added.

She told herself to ignore the voice. Yet even though her father had never been critical of her when she'd worked for him—not overtly critical, at least—she'd always known she wasn't quite measuring up to his expectations. She simply hadn't been good enough at certain aspects of the job.

Eliciting information from clients wasn't one of them, though. If Rachel had any idea about who might have killed Graham, even if it was buried deep in her subconscious, Anne was sure she could get at it.

Still, her father had connections she didn't, and if Chase hired him... Or why not have the best of both worlds?

There was no reason she couldn't ask her own father for advice about *anything*—including the best way to help her new neighbors. And as long as Chase wasn't officially Ben Barrett's client, if the cops came calling he'd be under no obligation to tell them a thing.

"So," Chase said quietly. "What's your advice? Even if there's a risk to using a private eye…"

She found herself reading his thoughts again. He wasn't going to ask her to get any more involved than she already was, but he desperately wanted her to.

Praying that she was doing the right thing, she said, "I think we should try to avoid the risk. At least for the time being, I think we should see where we can get on our own."

CHAPTER FIVE

ANNE LOCKED UP THE BACK of her house—aware she still wasn't used to the fact that it really was *hers*—then turned toward the pool.

Chase had gotten the girls out of the water, and while they were toweling themselves dry he headed along the edge and collected their flip-flops. He seemed so much like the sort of devoted dad her own had been that watching him sent her thoughts skittering back to her childhood.

She hadn't appreciated it then, but as an adult she realized single parenting was a tough job. And for someone like her father, whose hours were routinely unpredictable, even arranging day care would have been a major challenge.

Chase was lucky he could work at home part of the time. And that he had Rachel living with them.

She was curious about how they'd arrived at their arrangement. And even more curious, she silently admitted, about what had gone wrong between him and his wife. He didn't strike her as a man any sane woman would walk out on.

Of course, given what Julie had said, the obvious explanation was that her mother had decided a career was more important than a husband and child.

But obvious explanations weren't always the right ones. So maybe something else entirely had caused the breakup, and she'd moved to L.A. after it.

Anne glanced over to where Chase was standing with Julie. He was telling her that the two of them were going next door to talk to Rachel some more.

"Does that mean you haven't figured out what to do yet?" she asked anxiously.

"No, we've pretty much got it nailed down. We just need to discuss a few things. So don't start worrying again, okay?"

"'Kay," Julie slowly agreed.

A moment later, she smiled over and said, "Thanks a lot for the swim."

It was only then that Anne realized Chase had silently prompted her.

"Yeah, thanks, it was fun," Becky added.

"Good. We'll have to do it again soon."

"What have you two got planned for after you change?" Chase asked them.

"Mmm…call on Carol?" Becky suggested to Julie. "I bet her mom'd let us play with their kittens again."

"'Kay. But we better not tell her we were swimming."

Chase grinned. "She'd never guess from your wet hair."

"Right," Julie said. "Blow-dryers," she added to Becky.

They'd taken about two steps toward the gate when Becky yelled, "Race you to get ready!"

Anne watched them accelerate like a couple of human Indy cars, thinking they had more energy than ten adults.

"Having your best friend live next door must be great," she said as she and Chase headed after them.

"It's great for me, too. Her parents are terrific, and we can almost always manage trade-offs."

"Rachel's around most of the time, though?" she asked, hoping she sounded interested, not nosy.

"Right. I guess Julie mentioned I'm divorced?"

"Yes." She managed to stop there, telling herself that if he wanted to fill her in on the details, he would.

"Well, after my wife and I split, I needed someone who could be here when I wasn't. Rachel was just finishing university at the time, and she didn't have a job—but she wanted to stay in Toronto rather than go back to Peterborough. That's where we were raised."

"Ah," Anne said, her thoughts lingering on the "after my wife and I split" part of what he'd said. Surely there was an innocuous way of asking *why* they had.

After thinking about that for a few seconds, she began to wonder what had her so curious about his marriage.

Not that she was trying to deny her attraction to him, but she'd never been the type to care much about details of a man's past. Especially not mere hours after she'd met him. Every significant relationship she'd ever had with a man had developed slowly.

"Are you?"

"Pardon?" Whatever he'd said, she'd completely missed it.

"I asked if you're originally from Toronto."

"Oh, yes, I grew up in Leaside."

"Then you probably don't realize how confining small towns can be. They're great for kids. But as time goes by, more and more people leave once they've finished school."

They'd reached the deck that stretched across the width of his house. Beyond it, the mostly glass back wall revealed an inviting-looking family room. Rather than sliding open the door into it, he turned toward her—apparently not in a hurry to end their conversation.

"At any rate, that's how Rachel ended up living here. She needed a place and I needed help with Julie. I've got more confidence now, but in the beginning I was pretty worried about how I'd cope with raising a little girl on my own."

Anne nodded. "And it would have been a lot harder without someone like Rachel. I know that firsthand. My mom died when I was two, so I don't remember a time when it wasn't just my father and me."

"He never remarried?"

"No. I was always terrified he would, though. Terrified he'd marry someone I hated, I mean. But I think I'd have been okay with a stepmother if I'd liked her. And it would have been a lot easier on him. After I hit twelve or thirteen…'' She paused, shaking her head. ''He'd probably have killed for a Rachel when I was a teenager.''

''Don't tell me things like that. I already live in fear of her leaving.''

''You think she might?''

''Well, eventually, she'll meet someone she wants to marry. And even if that's not any time soon, she has a friend who edits a magazine in Vancouver. He's always after her to move out there—says she's got a standing offer of regular assignments. One way or another, I'm sure she won't stay forever.''

''And she's been here for…?''

''About six years. Julie was three when she moved in.'' He slid the door open then, precluding further questions.

THE MOMENT CHASE walked into the family room with his arm around Rachel's shoulders, Anne frowned and shook her head—which was exactly how he'd figured she'd react.

Rachel's migraine had gotten so bad that he'd been tempted to just leave her upstairs in the silent darkness of her bedroom. The way things stood, though, they couldn't wait until she was feeling better. She didn't often get a full-blown migraine. But when she did, it might be gone the next morning or it might last for days.

As soon as he settled her into one of the easy chairs by the fireplace, she put her head in her hands and began massaging her temples. Feeling like an ogre, he sank onto the couch on the other side of the coffee table, next to Anne.

"We can't do this now," she whispered.

"We have to," he whispered back.

Before either of them could say another word, the door to the deck slid open and Julie and Becky came in.

Julie glanced anxiously at Rachel, then at him. "Becky told her mom that Rachel couldn't even swim 'cuz of her head," she said quietly. "And Mrs. Slater said I should have dinner there and sleep over. Is that okay?"

"*Please,* Mr. Nicholson?" Becky begged. "We're havin' lasagna, and my mom makes the best lasagna in the world."

"'Cept for Rachel," Julie said loyally. "So is it okay, Dad?"

"Sure," he said, silently blessing Helen Slater.

The whole street, if not the entire neighborhood, had to know that Rachel was Graham Lowe's suspect girlfriend. And a lot of people were probably dying to ask questions. But Helen hadn't asked a single one.

All she'd said was, "Joe and I feel just sick about this. And if there's anything at all we can do to help, you only have to ask."

Now she was helping without even being asked, and she couldn't have picked a better time. If Rachel told Anne and him anything worth following up on, doing it would be a lot easier with Julie next door for the night.

"I'm just gonna get some stuff," she was telling him. "Come on, Becky," she added, heading for the backstairs.

He waited until they were out of sight, then said, "You're all right, Rachel? Can we get started now?"

"Yes," she murmured, not opening her eyes.

"Okay, you're on," he told Anne.

She hesitated, obviously not wanting any part of this, but finally said, "Rachel, are you *sure* you're up to talking?"

"Yes. Just don't talk very loud."

Anne shot him a look that suggested he must torture small animals in his spare time, then focused on Rachel again.

"I'm afraid everything's kind of run together in my mind," she began. "So I'm not entirely sure where we'd gotten to before you came home. But, at this point, Chase and I are thinking that Graham's killer might have known him. And had a reason for wanting him dead.

"Can you think of anyone with a major grudge against him? Anyone who'd threatened him or he was worried about?"

Her eyes still closed, Rachel slowly licked her lips. "No," she replied at last. "I...sorry, it's really hard to concentrate when you've got one of these things, but I know he never talked about anyone being out to get him.

"That probably doesn't mean much, though. He

wouldn't have told me something like that. Wouldn't have wanted me to worry.''

"Right," Anne said. ''That makes sense. Still…okay, forget about specific people. Did he ever say anything…or did you ever just get a feeling he was in some sort of danger?"

Rachel opened her eyes to tiny slits and peered over at them. "He'd been working undercover for the past few months. I guess that always involves danger."

"Undercover?" Anne repeated, glancing at Chase. "You didn't tell me that."

"I didn't know. This is the first time she's mentioned it. And the media have only been referring to him as an off-duty police detective," he added, feeling as guilty as if he'd been intentionally withholding information—even though this really *was* the first he'd heard of it.

"I wasn't supposed to tell anyone," Rachel said. "So I didn't. Not even you, Chase."

"Wait a minute. The girls are coming back down," he said, hearing them.

"You remembered your toothbrush?" he asked when they appeared on the stairs.

Julie nodded.

"Okay, then come give me a hug and I'll see you in the morning."

"And by then you'll have *everything* all figured out, right?" she said, her glance flickering to Anne.

"We're doing our best," Anne told her.

She gave Chase his hug, said goodbyes to Anne and Rachel, then she and Becky were gone.

"Okay, where was I," Anne murmured. "Oh, I know. Rachel, what about the detectives who questioned you? Did you tell *them* you knew Graham was working undercover?"

"No. With them, I figured he'd get in trouble if they knew he'd told me, so…jeez, that was stupid, wasn't it. He was dead. What sort of trouble was I thinking he could get in? But, no, they didn't ask me about it and I didn't say anything."

"Okay," Anne said. "Why was he under? What kind of case was he working on?"

"I don't know."

"He didn't tell you *anything* about it?"

"No."

"Rachel, this could be important. His death might be related to that case."

There was a silence, then she murmured, "Sorry, but I really don't have a clue. He only told me he was going under because his hours would be more erratic than usual."

"Okay," Anne said again. Her tone hadn't changed, but frustration had crept into her expression.

"Dead end?" Chase asked quietly, his hopes sinking.

She gave him an unhappy shrug, then looked at his sister again. "Let's try a different angle. Had Graham been acting unusual lately? Did he—"

"Wait," Rachel interrupted.

Chase stopped breathing.

"There *is* something that might help."

His pulse skipped a couple of beats and he started breathing again.

"I wasn't thinking about the killer being someone Graham knew. Or having anything to do with his case. I was just thinking…mugger in the park…with a connection to a dirty cop. But maybe I was only thinking that way because Graham seemed afraid there was one."

"A dirty cop, you mean?" Anne said.

"Yes."

One glance told Chase that Anne hadn't followed that last bit any better than he had.

"Rachel, are you talking about in the park?" he said. "Did Graham see another cop there or something?"

"No. I'm talking about the case he was working on. I may not have known what it was about, but I had the feeling he figured there was a dirty cop involved somehow."

"Why?" Anne asked.

"Because he was keeping his information on disk. He didn't want it sitting in a computer at the division. He didn't even want it in his own computer—in his apartment.

"He said he was worried that someone would try to take a look-see. And I assumed the "someone" had to be another cop. I mean, I guess just about anyone can break into an apartment, but who would have access to a police computer? Only another cop. Doesn't that make sense?''

"Well…yes," Anne agreed. "But why did he tell you all that when he didn't tell you anything about the case itself?''

"He had to. He was asking me to hold on to a backup disk for him. And I wanted to know why before I agreed.''

"A disk of information about his case?'' Anne asked, every trace of frustration vanishing as Rachel nodded.

"Right. He was carrying the original around with him, which meant it was at risk of being damaged. So he gave me a copy, then he was exchanging it for an updated one every day or two.''

"Do you still have the last one he gave you?''

Chase held his breath, waiting for Rachel's answer. Surely, if she had the disk, it would help them.

"Yes," she said. "I've still got it and a few other things of his. I was driving my own car the night we broke up, so he didn't bring me home. But that was last weekend. The disk's way out-of-date by now.''

Even so, Chase thought, if they knew what Graham had been working on… Then he remembered they were merely pursuing a theory. And that Graham's death might not be even remotely related to his work.

"He always kept the most up-to-date disk with him?'' Anne was asking. "He'd have had it at the park?''

"I…yes, he was a creature of habit. It would have been in his pocket."

"And what about the most recent backup? Assuming he made one after last weekend, what would he have done with it? Hidden it in his apartment?"

"I don't know. He might have. Or he could have asked someone else to keep it for him."

Anne looked at Chase. "You have a computer here?"

He nodded. "Upstairs. In my office."

"Then let's see what's on Rachel's disk."

CHASE'S OFFICE WAS ENORMOUS, containing not only a large desk but two long tables—one almost completely covered with unrolled architectural drawings, the other serving as the construction site for a scale model of an office tower. Undoubtedly, Anne thought, the project Julie was helping with.

On the wall beside his desk were photographs of modern buildings—ones he'd designed, she imagined. But even though she tried to focus her attention on them, her gaze kept drifting to his computer.

Its little green power light was glowing, so all they'd have to do was pop in that disk and—

"Got it," he announced, breezing into the room with a disk in his hand.

She warned herself against expecting too much. It might not contain a thing that would help them.

On the other hand, it might give them everything they needed. And *that* possibility made it hard to keep her excitement in check.

"Is Rachel lying down again?" she asked as he hauled a second chair over to the desk.

He nodded. "I promised I'd tell her if we got anything useful."

Gesturing for her to sit, he added, "Do you get migraines?"

"No."

"Neither do I. But they apparently make people incredibly sensitive to light. So as much as she wants to know what we find, sitting in front of a computer screen right now would about kill her.

"Okay, let's do it," he added, rolling his chair in close beside Anne's.

She felt a hot jolt of awareness as his thigh came to rest against hers, and for a moment her senses were completely focused on the sea-breeze scent of his aftershave, the firmness of his flesh and his body heat seeping through her skin, mingling with her own.

Then he touched the mouse, the screen came to life, and the moment passed.

Her heartbeat accelerating, she watched him slide in the disk and hit a few keys.

"We're in luck," he said. "It's in Word, not some obscure software."

When a directory appeared, she glanced down the list of file names. "Let's start with Summary."

He brought up the file. Operation Plastic, the heading read.

Silently, she began to skim.

"So that's what his assignment was," Chase said

after a few seconds. "Infiltrating a credit-card counterfeiting ring."

"Uh-huh," she murmured. "A major one, from the look of things. Scroll down some."

"I'll print it out, too. Hell, why don't I just print *all* the files."

She nodded, then went back to reading as the printer started. She stuck with the screen; after a couple of minutes, Chase moved to the other side of the desk and began reading the pages the printer was spitting out.

Ninety minutes and eight files later, they'd completed a crash course in credit-card counterfeiting.

They knew a whole lot about both the technical process of making the cards and how a counterfeiting ring operates. They also knew how Graham had infiltrated one in Toronto.

Posing as a newcomer to town, he'd joined as a runner. One of the low-level members who made cash withdrawals against the cards and purchased expensive items, like fine jewelry and electronics equipment, which were then sold on the black market.

He'd documented a lot of facts, including where some of the copying equipment was located and the identities of an even dozen of the ring members—noting that the controlling members led seemingly normal lives. To their friends and neighbors, they were the sort of professional men you'd find in any upscale neighborhood or on any private golf course.

Graham had also included a note about the men in

charge taking care of "personnel problems" themselves.

That, Anne had thought as she read it, probably ruled out the possibility of a hit man. If Graham's death *was* related to this case, it would have been a member of the counterfeiting operation who'd pulled the trigger.

"I didn't spot anything about him suspecting a dirty cop's involved, did you?" Chase asked, glancing across the desk at her.

She shook her head. There were brief references to a few of the other officers working on the Operation Plastic task force, but nothing to indicate Graham had concerns about any of them.

"That might mean nothing, though," she said. "If he had no solid proof, only suspicions, he'd probably have just kept them in his head. Cops don't normally accuse another cop of being crooked unless they're sure of it."

"And if he thought he might be in danger from anyone, he didn't mention that, either."

"No. But don't forget this information's a week old. Who knows what could have happened in the few days before he was killed? Even so, if his murder had anything to do with this case, we've got a lot to go on."

Chase eyed her for a long moment. "Then why don't you look happier?"

"Because we still don't know whether it *did* have anything to do with the case."

"How do we find out?"

"We go visit our special adviser. And hope he can get us some inside information."

"Oh? And who's our special adviser?"

"Ben Barrett. My father."

RACHEL WAS STILL in her bedroom, not feeling even a little better, and after Chase gave her a quick rundown of what was on the disk she simply wanted to be left alone.

"Until tomorrow, at least," she said.

From past experience, he knew she was serious. Which meant that he and Anne wouldn't have to worry about her when they went to see Ben Barrett. But the minute Chase walked back into his office, Anne's expression told him she hadn't managed to set up a meeting.

"I couldn't reach him," she said. "I got his machine at the house and his voice mail at his cellphone number. I left messages on both, but my phone's not connected yet, so I had to just say I'd try him again later."

"Why don't you call back and leave him my cellular number." He jotted it down for her.

"It's almost five," he added, handing her the phone. "So you can take that home for the weekend. Most of the calls I get on it are business ones."

He turned toward the window as she began to punch in one of her father's numbers again—only then realizing that, with the back of the house in late-afternoon shadows, he could see her reflection in the glass before him.

He watched her pressing the final numbers on the phone, thinking this entire situation was downright surreal.

Two days ago, he and Rachel were leading a relatively routine existence. Yesterday, their lives had been turned upside down. And today, Julie had brought him together with a complete stranger who, within hours, had become central to—no, *critical* to—keeping the mess Rachel was in from escalating into a total disaster.

"I've got the machine again," she murmured.

He let his gaze linger on her reflection as she waited for her father's message to finish, aware he'd never before become so quickly dependent on *anyone,* let alone someone he'd known only briefly.

He'd never become attracted to anyone so fast, either. Not even to his ex-wife.

Oh, the first time he'd seen her, singing in a Yorkville club, he'd thought she was beautiful. But it had been in a detached sort of way—the way he'd think about some actress on the screen. Whereas with Anne...

He didn't understand how or why it had happened, but he had the strangest sense that something within her had reached out and connected with him.

And improbable as it might be, he felt as if he'd known her for a long, long time. Felt it so strongly that if he believed in reincarnation, he'd be convinced they'd had a relationship in a former life. Because in some inexplicable way, she seemed so intimately familiar....

"Dad, it's me again," she said into the phone.

While she continued on, leaving her message, he tried once more to figure out why—specifically—she struck such a responsive chord in him.

As far as the physical went, there was little figuring required. He merely had to look at her thick dark hair to imagine how silky it would feel to his touch, just had to think about kissing her to taste…

She'd taste like sweet, ripe fruit. He was certain of that. Cherries was his best guess. Of course, there was only one way to be sure.

Forcing his gaze from her image in the glass, he reminded himself that he was perfectly happy with his life the way it was. At least, the way it had been before he'd turned on the news yesterday morning.

Besides, getting involved with a woman whose house sat directly behind his would be a very bad idea. If things didn't work out, she'd be far too close for comfort.

"All set," she said once she'd finished leaving a second message at the other number. "We'll just have to hope he checks in soon. But you're sure it's okay if I take your phone home?"

Chase nodded, although, foolish as he knew it was, he didn't want her going home.

"I don't suppose there's anything more we can do till we've seen him?" he asked casually. "Nothing from those files we should follow up on while we're waiting?"

"No. I really want to talk to him first. He was a police detective for a long time before he went into business for himself. He still has friends on the force. And when a cop's been killed, word gets around about the details of the case.

"So whether those detectives are focusing primarily on Rachel or not, if there's evidence pointing in other directions Dad should be able to learn something about it. And if he suspects Graham's death might be linked to that case…"

"Well, if he does, we'll take things from there. But we don't want to start checking out people involved in a counterfeiting ring unless we're sure we have to. They won't be the nicest sort of guys."

"Right. Guess I wasn't thinking about that."

She gave him a smile, then turned and started across his office.

He followed along, honestly intending to simply walk her downstairs. But as he slid open the door to the deck, he found himself saying, "You know, I promised I'd help you arrange furniture. I'm still up to it if you are."

When she absently pushed back her hair, considering the idea, she looked so appealing that he jammed his hands in his pockets to keep from doing something incredibly stupid.

"How about a rain check?" she said. "I'm feeling kind of drained."

"Sure. Anytime."

He told himself that if he pressed even an inch further she'd think he was a total jerk, yet the very next second he was saying, "I'm feeling guilty, though. I mean, Rachel and I blew your entire day, so how about I buy you dinner? It's the least I can do.''

''Ah…thanks, but all I really want is a quick dip in the pool and a pizza delivered to my door. Which means it's a good thing you're lending me your phone.

''I promise not to let it fall in the water,'' she added, giving him another smile.

''Good. It works better dry.''

Trying to ignore both his disappointment and the urge to kick himself, he dug a business card out of his pocket and gave it to her. ''The last of those numbers is for my home office.''

''Fine. I'll talk to you after Dad calls.''

She took a backward step, then stopped and said, ''Unless you feel like a swim and a pizza?''

CHAPTER SIX

EYES HIDDEN BEHIND her sunglasses, her bare feet dangling in the shallow end of the pool, Anne watched Chase swim another lap.

She still wasn't sure why she'd invited him back here. And she knew it hadn't been the wisest move. But one second she'd been out the door, on her way home, and the next the invitation had simply popped out of her mouth.

Until that instant, she'd been telling herself she needed time alone. To figure out how it was possible that a man who'd barely walked into her life could already seem to belong there. And to decide what she should do about the fact.

After all, he came with complications. And she'd never really given any thought to the possibility of finding herself interested in a man who had a daughter.

But she liked children. More important, she liked *his* child. Julie was a real sweetheart. Besides, *all* men came with complications of one sort or another.

Glancing back toward the patio, to where he'd left his T-shirt and cutoffs when he'd stripped down to his swimming trunks, she realized that even his clothes seemed at home where he'd tossed them over her chair.

It gave her an eerie feeling, as if she were starring in a play and a new male lead had unexpectedly been written in.

When she glanced at Chase again, he'd reached the far end of the pool and was hoisting himself out—so effortlessly that she wondered if he was consciously trying to impress her. Whether he was or not, he was doing an excellent job of it.

Since he was facing away from her, she let herself have a good long look.

For a lean man, he had a lot of muscles. She didn't know the names of most of them, but they were all well developed and enticingly masculine. And the water glistening on his tanned skin only served to highlight them.

As he turned and picked up a towel, she decided he also had just the right amount of chest hair. The thought made her smile to herself, because, not surprisingly, her definition of "just right" was the exact amount she liked. Not too much but not too little.

Lord, thus far, she hadn't discovered anything about him she *didn't* like. Except, of course, that his sister might have killed Graham Lowe.

Wishing her concerns about Rachel's guilt hadn't resurfaced, she tried to stop them in their tracks—but couldn't. Then a new question began nagging at her. If, in trying to prove Rachel innocent they found proof she was guilty, would Chase want to bury the evidence?

He struck her as too decent a man to even consider doing that under most circumstances. But when it came to someone he loved, she had a feeling he might want to play by different rules. And if so, they'd be coming at the issue from completely different directions.

She'd feel bound to turn over *whatever* evidence they found to the police. She was too much her father's daughter to do anything else and maintain even a shred of self-respect. So that was what she'd have to do, regardless of how it affected her relationship with Chase.

But she was getting way ahead of herself. In the first place, she'd decided the odds of Rachel being guilty were low. And in the second place, she and Chase had known each other so briefly that they had nothing more than the most superficial of "relationships."

Still, a deeper one could develop. She had little doubt of that—not when every time he was within touching distance she could feel electricity in the air between them. And from the way he kept eyeing her, she knew he felt it, too.

Yet the last thing this situation needed was one more complication. So until she was certain that Graham had been alive and well when Rachel left him…

Glancing at Chase once more, she mentally etched the word *platonic* into her mind. That was the only way to play this—for the time being, at least.

Besides, in due course she might start discovering all kinds of things about him that she didn't like.

Although she had a strong feeling that wouldn't happen.

She watched him start along the edge of the pool toward her, combing his fingers through his wet hair as he walked. And absurd as it seemed, she could actually feel her heart begin beating faster.

Once he'd reached her, he lowered himself down onto the edge of the pool beside her—and her heart began positively racing.

"Will you be hiring a company to look after the pool?" he asked.

"I don't think so. My real estate woman said there's nothing to it."

He grinned.

It made her wonder what kissing him would be like. He had a very sensual mouth.

"Your real estate woman's definition of 'nothing' isn't quite the same as mine," he told her. "Whenever there's much breeze, those aspens drop a lot of leaves. Peter Kitchner used to be out here skimming at least every other day.

"You've got to keep an eye on the chemical balance, too. If it's out of whack, you end up with algae. And I won't even get into the work of opening and closing for the season."

"Oh." She gazed at the water for a few seconds, then looked at Chase again.

"While I was growing up, I used to beg my father for a pool. But he'd always tell me they were too much work. I guess I convinced myself he was only saying that."

When Chase laughed, she realized it was the first time she'd heard his laugh. It was rich and deep, the kind that invites other people to laugh along.

"Must be a standard father's line," he said. "Julie would love a pool, but that's exactly what I keep saying. They're too much work.

"Actually, when I... Your real estate agent told Mavis Kitchner that you'd be living here alone, and when I heard that I wondered if you knew what you were getting into.

"I don't mean to sound sexist," he added quickly. "It's just that, even aside from the pool, something always seems to need fixing around a house, and most women were never taught...

He paused, shaking his head. "I'm just getting myself in deeper here, aren't I. And for all I know, you're a whiz at home repairs."

"No, I'm definitely not a whiz. I can use the basic tools, but that's it. I don't like apartment living, though. I've been in one for the past few years, and I just..."

She shrugged, thinking this was as good a time as any to mention that she was divorced—although she suspected he already knew, courtesy of her real estate agent and Mavis Kitchner.

"My marriage broke up about three years ago, and we sold our house," she explained. "The apartment I rented was nice enough, but I missed having a yard. And I...oh, there were a lot of reasons for wanting a house again."

"Well, I hope I didn't start you wondering if buying this one was a mistake. As far as I know there's nothing wrong with it—except that it's got a pool, of course,'' he teased.

''Yes, I could see how much you hated swimming in it. Maybe I'd better think about filling it in.''

That made him laugh again, and she couldn't help smiling. She liked a man who appreciated her sense of humor.

Chase looked down the length of the pool, hesitating. Rachel was always telling him he was even worse than most men when it came to bluntness.

But he'd always found that if he wanted to know something, the easiest way to find out was to ask a question. And right this minute, sitting here so close to Anne that he was far more aware of her than he'd prefer to be, there was something he wanted to know.

Maybe he hadn't been looking for a relationship. And maybe getting into one with her would be a bad idea. But he still wanted to know.

''Would I be out of line to ask what happened?'' he said. ''To your marriage, I mean? I'm just curious, because you strike me as pretty easygoing.''

She slowly pushed her sunglasses up onto her head and eyed him.

After three seconds of gazing into the dark depth of her eyes, he couldn't, for the life of him, recall why he'd thought getting into a relationship with her would be a bad idea. In fact, there was something so utterly tantalizing about her that he wanted to just wrap his arms around her and never let her go.

''Well…'' she said slowly, ''I'm not sure whether

the basic problem was that I changed or that Tom—my husband—didn't want me to. You see, when we met I was working for my dad, and Tom liked that. He saw it as a good, safe—"

"Safe?" Chase interrupted before he could catch himself. "That's not a word I'd think of to describe being a P.I."

Anne shook her head. "It's nowhere near as dangerous as people think—except in the movies. In real life, there's rarely anything to worry about. In fact, most cases are downright boring. You sit for hours in a car, watching a house, or spend days following paper trails.

"But I guess *safe* wasn't the best word to use. I should have said that Tom saw it as a *secure* job.

"I made good money, and working for my father meant I wasn't likely to ever get fired. Actually, Tom just assumed I'd eventually take over the business, because my father was calling it Barrett and Barrett at the time—one reason I didn't change my name when I got married. At any rate, Tom liked all those things.

"But, not long after our wedding, I realized that being a P.I. wasn't what I really wanted.

"I'd already been writing for a few years. I wasn't published yet, but I'd begun submitting manuscripts and I was hoping. Because the more writing I did, the more I loved it. For Tom, though, it was a real problem."

"He resented the time?"

"Exactly. He didn't want me sitting at a computer.

He wanted me doing things with him, even if it was just watching something on TV that I had no interest in.

"Plus, the thought of me actually quitting a 'terrific job' as he called it, to try to make a living as a writer…"

"You wanted to do what made you happy, though."

"Right. So, after I sold my first book, I told my father I wanted to write full-time. He was hurt that I would quit, but he took it a lot better than Tom did. From then on, things just kept getting worse between us.

"When you're a brand-new author, you don't exactly have a steady stream of income and…"

She paused, shaking her head. "I'm sounding as if I think he was totally to blame, and I don't mean to.

"I know I wasn't the same woman he'd married, and that he felt as if I'd rewritten the rules when he didn't want me to. But if only he'd made an effort to understand, instead of putting all his energy into trying to keep me just the way I was…

"I guess there's never much point to 'if onlys,' though, is there. What happened, happened. And what we had in the beginning was long gone by the time I moved out."

"Ah," Chase said quietly, gazing over the pool once more.

He was almost sorry he'd asked his question, because her explanation had left him with a hollow feeling in his chest.

Oh, he could see how, as she'd said, neither she nor this Tom had been completely to blame. But they'd broken up because being a writer was more important to her than her husband. And that had a painfully familiar ring to it.

"Do I get a turn?" she said quietly.

He looked at her again.

"Julie told me your ex-wife's a singer. And she lives in L.A. That's all I know."

"Yeah...well, there's not much else *to* know. Yvonne didn't change. She was a singer when we met. Unfortunately, she married me and had Julie before she realized we weren't what she wanted most."

"Sorry," Anne murmured.

He shrugged. "I've been over it for a long time."

And it had taught him a valuable lesson—that some women leave their husbands because other things are more important.

Just as well, he told himself, he'd learned at this stage of the game that Anne was one of those women. But just as well or not, he still felt hollow inside.

JULY DAYS LAST FOREVER in Toronto, so even though it was almost eight by the time Chase and Anne finished their pizza, the daylight hadn't begun to fade.

"I guess I should head home," he said, pushing his chair back from the patio table.

"Sure, you must want to see if Rachel's okay."

He shook his head. "When she's got a full-blown migraine she'd rather just be left alone. But it doesn't look as if your dad's going to get back to you tonight," he added, glancing at his cell phone.

"Oh, he probably will. He works out of the house, so even if he doesn't call in for messages he'll check them as soon as he gets home. The only question is when that'll be. But if it's not too late… Or would you rather just leave seeing him until tomorrow?"

"No," he said quickly. "If we still get a chance to go there tonight, let's do it."

"Okay, then I'll phone you later. Or if you want to wait here a little longer, I could make more lemonade."

"Well…yeah, that sounds good," he said, even though he knew he'd be a lot smarter to leave.

They were both fully dressed again. But he couldn't stop picturing Anne nearly naked in her black bikini. No matter how many times he managed to force the image away, a few minutes later he was seeing it again. And each time he did, he had more trouble remembering that there was absolutely no way he intended to get involved with her.

However, the mental picture was nothing more than normal male fantasizing. Whereas the real thing…

He followed her with his gaze as she headed for the house, aware that something about her walk made it almost impossible to keep from watching her. The way her hips moved wasn't exactly provocative, but...

When he couldn't think of a better word to describe it, he decided he shouldn't be trying. Now that he knew she wasn't a woman who took commitment seriously....

After his thoughts drifted down that path a bit, he began to wonder if something had short-circuited in his brain.

He wasn't looking for commitment. So why should he care whether Anne Barrett had chosen her writing over her husband? Hell, why should he care if she'd chosen it over six husbands?

In fact, he should probably be *glad* she was the way she was. Then, if they did happen to get involved in some temporary thing, he wouldn't have to worry about her being too close for comfort after it was over.

Leaning back in his chair, he considered that for a minute, feeling vastly relieved.

He'd obviously just been suffering from a temporary lapse of sanity. Because wasn't a woman who didn't want commitment every man's dream? He was in the midst of assuring himself it was when his phone rang.

"Chase Nicholson," he answered.

There was a moment's silence before a man asked, "Is this 555-2532?"

"Yes. Mr. Barrett?"

"Right. Is my daughter still at this number?"

"Yes, she is. Just one second and I'll get her."

Not that "getting" was actually necessary. Anne was already halfway across the patio, carrying a fresh pitcher of lemonade.

"Your father," he said, extending the cellular to her.

She set down the pitcher and took the phone. "Hi, Dad, are you calling from home?... Well, I wonder if I could come over and talk to you about something.... Uh-huh, as long as *now's* okay with you.... No, nothing's wrong. It's just that the man who answered is one of my new neighbors, and he's got a problem we could use your advice about.... Uh-huh, *we*. I'm going to bring him along in case you have questions I can't answer.... Great. We'll leave right now. See you in half an hour or so."

IF SOMEONE HAD ASKED Chase to pick Anne's father out of a crowd, one of his last choices would have been Ben Barrett.

He didn't bear the slightest resemblance to his daughter. His eyes were blue and his hair, although beginning to gray, was still a sandy color.

In his late fifties, solidly built and sporting a full mustache, he looked like a mean ex-football tackle. But his welcome was warm, and when he led them into his office—saying they'd talk there because he was half expecting a call—there wasn't a football trophy to be seen.

After he'd gestured them to the conversation area

on one side of the room, Chase pretty much just listened while Anne told the story.

Occasionally, her father directed a question his way, but it was obvious the two of them had worked together on a lot of cases and had developed a kind of verbal shorthand he didn't know.

"So that's where we are," Anne finally concluded. "And I thought that if you wouldn't mind talking to a few of your buddies on the force, you might be able to fill in some of the blanks for us—maybe find out if Graham's wallet and that disk were on his body. And whether there were any signs of a struggle. Because if not, if the guy who called Chase fabricated that part, I just don't understand how those detectives could think Rachel was involved."

"I see," Ben said. Then he turned to Chase. "You're dead set against reporting that extortion call?"

"Dad, I explained why they decided not to," Anne said before Chase could open his mouth.

"You should," Ben told him. "But if you don't, what are you going to do when he calls again?"

This time, Chase had an answer. He and Anne had talked about his options over dinner.

"I'll try to stall him," he said. "Say it's going to take me a while to come up with so much money."

"And if that doesn't work?"

"Then I guess, if he makes good on his threat, if he does try to incriminate Rachel, we'll just have to count on the cops seeing through it."

He hoped Ben would tell him they probably

would, but all he said was, "Well, when you try to buy your time, ask for as much as possible. Because you might be able to pull it off once, but he probably won't go for it twice."

"I'll keep that in mind."

"Do you think a recorder would be a good idea?" Anne said.

"Yeah, I do. I'll lend you one that you can attach to your office phone," he told Chase. "It'll automatically record conversations. And this guy might say something that'll be useful to have on tape.

"But what about your sister?" he continued. "You don't believe there's any chance she actually shot this man? Not even accidentally?"

"No. No way in the world."

Ben looked skeptical. "Even if she wouldn't normally lie to you, if she's afraid enough of where telling the truth would get her…"

"The only thing she's afraid of is being railroaded."

He merely nodded in response to that, which made Chase doubt he was completely convinced of Rachel's innocence. But that was hardly surprising when the detectives handling the case weren't—not by a long shot.

"Have you talked to a lawyer?" Ben asked next.

Chase shook his head. "We thought about it. But then my daughter got Anne involved and… You think we should?"

"I wouldn't say it's critical at this point. But you should have one lined up. If those detectives decide to take Rachel in for further questioning, you don't want to be suddenly scrambling for someone half-decent.''

A chill seized Chase. Ben might have said *if* they decided to take Rachel in for further questioning, but his tone had said *when*.

''Would you like me to make a few calls for you?'' he asked. ''Find a good one who could likely free up some time if you need it?''

''I'd really appreciate that.''

After a few seconds of silence, Anne said, ''What do you think about how we have things figured?''

''Well, I'd say you've definitely nailed the three most likely possibilities. Odds are, it's either a random killing, a tie-in to the case Graham was working on or some motive we don't know about.

''If that's it, and I ask around a little, I might hear something. As for a random killing, I agree that's the least probable. I think we have to assume the shooter knew Graham. Or that he's in cahoots with someone who did. As you said, since the extortionist was aware who Rachel was, and that he'd be smarter to try getting money from Chase, here...''

Ben paused, then slowly nodded. ''You know, the more I think about the murder being connected to that case, the more it seems to add up.

''If Graham was nervous enough about somebody looking at his notes that he wasn't storing them on his hard drive, there was obviously something strange going on. Then he gets killed. It could just be a coincidence, but that's not what my gut's telling me. And if one of the ring members made him as a cop, they'd have killed him in a New York minute.

"So what about their names?" he asked. "How many are in those files?"

"Twelve," Anne told him. "And it's more than just names. We've got dates of birth, social insurance numbers and addresses. For some, there's other stuff, as well. But you can't think of anything more than those three possibilities? Nothing I missed?"

"Why would you have missed anything?" Ben said, shooting her a grin. "You were trained by the best."

Chase glanced at Anne, checking her reaction to her father's teasing.

She gave Ben a small smile, then said, "That may be true, but I don't have your contacts. So…will you see what you can find out for us?"

He didn't immediately reply, which gave Chase a horrible feeling the answer was going to be no.

"Darling, how far do you figure on taking this?" was what he finally said.

"What do you mean?"

"I mean you personally. How far are you thinking of taking it yourself? After all, we're talking about trying to ID a murderer."

"Well…yes. But as I explained, we decided it wouldn't be smart to actually hire a P.I. when Chase and Rachel aren't telling the police about—"

"Anne," Ben interrupted. "If the killer gets wind of what you're up to, what do you think he'll do? Regardless of whether he's a member of that counterfeiting operation, or just someone who had a hate on for Graham, or…''

When Ben paused, slowly shaking his head, it suddenly struck Chase that the idea of him and Anne pursuing this any further on their own might be positively insane.

What had she said earlier? Her words readily came back to him: *We don't want to start checking out people involved in a counterfeiting ring unless we're sure we have to. They won't be the nicest sort of guys.*

Why hadn't he recognized that as a colossal understatement when she'd said it? And even if the killer wasn't a ring member, he was still a killer who wouldn't want to be caught.

''Anne, tracking down a murderer isn't your job,'' Ben was saying. ''That's what those police detectives are getting paid to do. So have Rachel hand over the disk to them, in case they don't have the most recent one, and let *them* decide if they think Graham's death could be related to what he was working on.

''Sorry,'' he added, looking at Chase. ''I know you want to help your sister. But you've got a daughter of your own, so you'll understand where I'm coming from here.''

''Dad, I've already told Chase and Rachel that I'm going to help,'' Anne said, her voice not quite even.

''But your father's right,'' Chase told her. ''If the killer found out what we were doing… Hell, I don't know what I was thinking, why it didn't strike me before now that…'' His words trailed off when he saw that Anne was staring at him as if he were a traitor.

"You were thinking about your sister being charged with murder," she said. "And that the way to ensure it doesn't happen is to ID the real killer.

"Dad, I'm not a child," she continued, turning back to Ben. "I won't do anything stupid. But I promised I'd try to help and I intend to."

"Dammit, Anne, how did I end up with the most stubborn daughter in the free world?"

"Genetics would be my best guess," she said wryly. "But if you'd rather not see what you can find out for us, just say so and I'll ask someone else. Rachel knows a lot of cops. Friends of Graham's. And I'm sure one of them would give us a hand."

"And what if, by unlucky coincidence, your 'one of them' turned out to be this dirty cop Rachel figures is somehow involved?"

Chase glanced at Anne and his heart gave an uneasy thud.

She looked as if that possibility hadn't occurred to her any more than it had to him. But it *could* happen. So if Ben decided he wasn't going to help them and they took this any further, they'd have even more to worry about than they'd been thinking.

"Maybe there isn't any dirty cop," Anne was saying. "Rachel only thinks there might be."

When Ben said nothing in reply, Chase's thoughts began to race.

With her father implying that things could get far too dangerous and Anne saying she wouldn't let them, he assumed the truth lay somewhere in the middle. And if he could help Rachel without *serious* danger of Anne and him ending up in major trouble, he desperately wanted to.

On the other hand, as her father was saying, this was no game of Clue. They'd be trying to track down a real, live cop killer.

"I'll tell you what," Ben said at last. "I'll ask around if you agree to a couple of conditions."

"What conditions?" Anne demanded.

"If I find out any useful information, we discuss what you're going to do with it before you do it. And you keep me informed every step of the way. Deal?"

She looked at Chase.

His immediate impulse was to tell her that of course they wanted her father involved. Under just about *any* conditions.

Aside from the two-heads-are-better rule, she'd said he was one of the best in the business. So he'd know if they started getting themselves in too deep.

Something in her expression, though, warned him not to say any of that.

"Whatever you think," he finally said. "You're the expert, not me."

CHAPTER SEVEN

DARKNESS HAD FALLEN by the time Chase and Anne left her father's house and climbed back into Chase's Cherokee. She was silent during the drive home. He spent it trying to convince himself he should ask what was bothering her.

Not any better at emotional stuff than most men, he'd prefer to just keep pretending he didn't realize she was upset. Yet, considering how much he owed her, if there was anything he could do to help he should. But what if he said the wrong thing and only made matters worse?

He was still feeling ambivalent when he turned onto her street. Unless he'd completely misread things, the problem stemmed from her father's insistence on being involved in their "case," for lack of a better word—involved, at least, beyond seeing what he could find out for them.

Where things got foggy, to Chase's way of thinking, was why that would bother Anne as much as it seemed to be doing. After all, asking Ben for help had been *her* idea, so surely she shouldn't resent...

Of course, she couldn't have liked his telling her she had to keep him informed and such, as if she still worked for him. But she had to know him well enough that it wouldn't have surprised her. So what was the big deal?

Pulling into her driveway, he told himself that if he was going to speak up it had to be soon.

"It's been a long day, hasn't it," she said, giving him a wan smile.

He nodded. "And I really appreciate everything you've done. Without you…hell, without you, I'd be no further ahead than I was this morning.

"Let's just hope my father learns something that gets us a lot further yet. And you'll hook up that recorder tonight?"

"Uh-huh."

"Good. Then I'll talk to you as soon as I hear from him. Or call me if anything happens on your side of the fence."

"Anne?" he said as she reached for the door handle.

When she glanced back, a moonbeam straying through the windshield painted her hair silver, making her look downright ethereal.

He felt a sudden urge to kiss her, struggled to ignore it, but failed miserably. It was far too strong to ignore. He was going to resist it, though. That was the important thing.

"What's wrong?" he asked.

"Nothing."

"No? You've been so quiet, I was sure…"

Anne almost said she was just tired, then didn't. She usually kept her feelings to herself, but if something was still bothering her when she went to bed she always had trouble sleeping. So maybe she should talk a little. Or would she only end up wishing she hadn't?

She wasn't sure. She certainly found Chase easy enough to talk to. And they somehow seemed to have packed a year of getting to know each other into a single day. Even so, if she confided in him he'd probably think she was overly sensitive. And she wasn't. She simply—

"I'm not the world's best listener," he said quietly. "But I'm not the worst, either."

He turned off the ignition, the glow of the dashboard lights vanished, and the night wrapped itself more darkly around them. She could still see him watching her, though, and she could feel temptation curling low in her belly.

She wanted to kiss him. And if she made the slightest move toward him, she knew he'd take her in his arms. But as tempted as she was, she simply said, "You'll think it's really silly."

He smiled, making her want to kiss him even more.

"I'm used to hearing about a nine-year-old's problems," he said. "I doubt you could come close to some of those for silly. So…?"

"I…" She hesitated. Then she told herself to just get it over with, and the rest of the words came rushing out. "My feelings are hurt because my dad doesn't figure I'm up to helping you and Rachel."

"What?"

She shrugged, aware her face was flushed and hoping the night would hide it. "I knew you'd think it was silly."

"But…that's not what I'm thinking. I'm just wondering why you figure he doesn't."

He looked sincerely puzzled, although she didn't know how he possibly could be.

"You were there," she reminded him. "You heard him say I should leave the case to the cops. That I shouldn't try to take things any further. And when I told him I intended to, he attached strings to his helping. Now, unless I want to go back on my word, we won't make a move without running it by him first. What does all that add up to in your mind?"

"Anne…obviously you know him a whole lot better than I do, but I didn't read any criticism into what he said. Practically the first thing he told you was that you had everything figured out."

She simply shrugged again. "Figuring out" and "doing" were two different things.

"He just knew he'd be worried about you if you got in any deeper," Chase continued.

"Because I wouldn't be up to the job."

"No. All I heard was fatherly concern. Nothing else. You're his daughter. He loves you. And I didn't get *any* sense that he was afraid you weren't up to the job. He was just focusing more on the potential danger than we'd been.

"It was the way I'd feel if…say, Rachel took Julie to New York City. I'd worry while they were gone, but not because I'd think either of them would do something stupid. I'd be worried about the crazy cab-bies and the crack-heads on the street.''

''I…you're not just saying that? You really didn't think my dad…''

''Anne, he even said I'd understand because I have a daughter of my own. And he was right. He worries about you the way I worry about Julie.''

''But I'm an adult.''

''I don't think that matters. You're still his daugh-ter.''

''Well…''

She thought about that for a few moments, then silently admitted that she just might have misread her father's reaction. Not entirely, but a little. Maybe, even if he figured her investigative skills were top-notch, he'd worry.

He didn't think they were, of course, but she wouldn't bother telling Chase that. His confidence in her would nose-dive if she admitted she'd never been anywhere near as good a P.I. as her father.

''Feel any better?''

''Yes.'' She managed a smile. ''If the architecting business ever dries up, you can go into counseling.''

When he smiled, she realized she was back to wanting him to kiss her. And for a moment she was certain he was going to.

Then he gestured to where his cellular phone was sitting on the console between the seats, and said, ''Don't forget to take that. I told your dad you'd have it all weekend.''

''Thanks,'' she murmured, forcing away her disappointment by telling herself he must have decided the same thing she had—that keeping their relationship platonic was the only way to go.

She'd just have to do a better job of remembering.

ALMOST THE FIRST THING Anne saw when she woke up in the morning was Chase's cellular—sitting where she'd left it on the bedside table. And seeing it reminded her about that final conversation with her father last night.

He'd phoned just as she was climbing into bed, to ask how convinced she was that Rachel Nicholson hadn't actually killed Graham Lowe. Obviously, his gut feeling that the murder was related to the counterfeiting case wasn't enough to make him completely rule out Rachel as a suspect.

And he hadn't been happy to hear that his daughter wasn't one hundred percent convinced of Rachel's innocence, either. Not even though she'd assured him she was close to certain Rachel was telling the truth.

"And what's going to happen if it turns out she did it?" he'd demanded—the very question, of course, that Anne had been asking herself.

It was as close as he'd come to saying she shouldn't have gotten involved with the Nicholsons' problems. But it had been close enough to start her second-guessing herself again. If Rachel was lying, if that was what she and Chase ended up learning, she'd be wishing with all her might that she'd steered clear of their situation.

But by this point, both Chase and Rachel—and

Julie, as well—were counting on her. She couldn't back off now, so she'd just have to pray that Rachel was as innocent as she claimed.

Assuring herself that was undoubtedly the case, she climbed out of bed and began getting organized. After she'd made it downstairs and put the coffee on, she checked outside the front door—and sure enough, a copy of the Saturday *Globe and Mail* was there.

Thinking the people at the newspaper were far quicker about getting her reconnected to the world than were the ones who worked for the phone company, she took the paper, a mug of coffee and Chase's cellular phone out to the patio.

Not that she really expected her father would have anything to report until far later, if he got back to her today at all. Still, he'd surprised her before.

After glancing at the morning's headlines, she tried to immerse herself in the Arts section. But her gaze kept straying over the fence to Chase's house.

There was no sign of activity, which started her imagining him in bed—his dark hair disheveled on the pillow, a rumpled sheet pulled up barely to his waist, morning stubble making his face look...

"Oh, for heaven's sake, stop it," she muttered.

She was a thirty-two-year-old woman, not a sixteen-year-old. So why was she feeling like a lovesick teenager? Not to mention acting like one.

She'd never admit it to a soul, but she'd spent fifteen minutes searching through cartons for her favorite shorts and top, then had gone to the effort of ironing them. And try as she might, she couldn't manage to stop thinking about Chase Nicholson for more than three seconds straight.

He'd even been wandering around in her dreams last night. In his bathing trunks, no less. And he'd looked so darned sexy that her hand had developed a mind of its own—reaching out and tracing his chiseled jaw with her fingertips. The next instant, he'd vanished into mist.

Wondering what a Freudian would make of that, she forced her gaze back to the article she'd started to read. She only got through another few lines before the phone rang.

She picked it up, expecting to hear her father's voice. Instead, it was Chase calling. When he said hello, her heart skipped a beat.

"Anne, do you think you could come over here?" he asked, his tone quiet but urgent. "I can see you're in the middle of coffee, but... I wasn't watching you," he quickly added. "I just glanced over as I dialed."

She looked up toward his office and, sure enough, he was at the window.

He raised a hand in greeting.

Feeling incredibly self-conscious, she waved, then mentally scrambled back through the past few minutes, praying she hadn't scratched herself in an embarrassing place or anything since he'd been standing there.

"We've got company," he continued, still gazing at her. "At least, Rachel has. And, fortunately, she's over her migraine, because we need her thinking straight.

"If she's right about there being a dirty cop, this guy could be it. He's a police detective, a friend of Graham's."

"What does he want?"

"I'm not sure. Ostensibly, he's on his way to work and just stopped by to see if she's doing okay. But how many people *just stop by* before nine in the morning? So I thought you should be here—that if he's got a hidden agenda, the more of us trying to figure out what it is the better."

"Good thinking. And if we can get him talking about the murder, maybe we'll learn something. I'll be there in two seconds."

"No, wait."

She waited, not taking her eyes off Chase.

"He'd figure a neighbor just wandering over and joining in was pretty strange. So how about we pretend we've got something going?"

"Good idea."

"And give me longer than two seconds. I want to call next door—ask Helen Slater to keep Julie there until this guy's gone. Then I'll have to drag Rachel away from him and explain what we're doing."

"Right. Is ten minutes enough?"

"Should be lots."

"What about your cell phone?"

"Just leave it there. I've got voice mail. If your dad calls, we'll know."

"Okay, see you in a few minutes."

"Good. And thanks."

As Chase turned away from the window, she clicked the phone off, thinking that *pretending* to have something going with him would hardly tax her acting skills.

The lyrics of Bonnie Raitt's "Something to Talk About" drifting through her mind, she drank a little more coffee and checked on whether the Blue Jays had beaten the Rangers last night. Then, after taking the paper and phone back into the house, she headed for the Nicholsons'.

"ANNE'S ON HER WAY OVER," Chase said, interrupting Dave Hustis midsentence as she started across the backyard.

"Anne's our neighbor," Rachel explained. "She's also my brother's…what should I call her?"

She shot Chase a teasing smile. It was shaky, but genuine-enough looking to let him relax a little. Upset as she still was, she was obviously determined to do her part.

He smiled back at her, letting Dave draw the obvious conclusion about his relationship with Anne, then he headed over to slide the door open for her. When she stepped into the family room, he wrapped his arm around her shoulders and kissed her cheek.

One breath of her perfume, one second with his lips touching the smooth warmth of her skin, and all he could think about was making love with her—in a field of wildflowers. Slow love under a hot sun and blue sky.

Telling himself that was *not* what he needed to be thinking about at the moment, he introduced her to Dave, trying to see their visitor through her "investigator" eyes as the man rose from his chair and extended his hand.

But Dave still looked like nothing other than an average guy in his early thirties, about six feet tall, with a medium build and brown hair. The kind of man who'd fade into a crowd.

"Dave and Graham were friends," Rachel was saying to Anne.

"Oh. I'm sorry. I didn't mean to interrupt anything, so why don't I just—"

"Why don't you just sit down," Chase said, taking her hand and leading her to the couch.

"I've been crying on Anne's shoulder so much it's a wonder she hasn't washed away," Rachel told Dave.

He glanced at Anne.

"That's what friends are for," she said.

Nodding, he turned toward Rachel once more. "Well, as I was saying, if there's anything I can do to help, be sure and let me know."

"Maybe there *is* something," Chase interjected.

"Anything," Dave repeated, turning to him. "Just name it."

"The two detectives investigating Graham's murder—"

"Brian Westin and Daryl Providence. I know them. They're good guys."

"I guess they probably are. But they've got Rachel pegged as their prime suspect."

Dave slowly shook his head. "I don't think you really have anything to worry about there. All that stuff on the news, implying Graham's girlfriend is a suspect—that's just media hype. Those reporters are a bunch of jackals. You can *never* believe what you hear on TV."

"I realize that," Chase told him. "But Westin and Providence were here for a long time on Thursday. And both Rachel and I are sure they figured she was…well, as I said, if they aren't totally convinced she's the one who killed Graham, she's at least their prime suspect."

"Really," Dave said slowly. "I…the guys are talking, of course. They always do when there's a case involving another cop. But I figured—"

"You mean the *police* grapevine's saying I did it?" Rachel interrupted anxiously.

"Well…cops are the same as everyone else. We see stuff on the news and even though we should know better…but most of us don't really have a lot more insight into the investigation than you do."

"You mean not a lot but *some* more?" Anne asked with a wide-eyed, innocent expression. It suggested she'd be impressed as hell if he gave her an example of something he knew.

But all he said was "Not really. I haven't heard anything more than a few in-house rumors."

"Aside from the rumors saying *I* did it, you mean?" Rachel asked, clearly even more upset.

Dave shrugged uncomfortably. "Rumors are only rumors. But there's one thing you could do, although I'm not sure it's the greatest idea."

"What's that?" Chase asked.

"Well, have you considered hiring a private investigator?"

"No," he lied. "Do you think we should?"

"Not really. It's just that I can see how worried Rachel is. And if you had someone with only her interests in mind… I mean, if it would make you feel better," he added, looking at Rachel again.

"Is there anyone you'd recommend?" Anne asked.

Dave shook his head. "Actually, I'm not even recommending the idea. I've seen those guys just get in the way too often. And, really, it would probably be a waste of money.

"The Homicide guys almost never charge the wrong person. Their cases are high-profile, and none of them wants his ass to be grass. Besides, they'll want the *real* killer. They wouldn't try to pin Graham's death on someone just to close the case.

"But I'll tell you what," he added to Rachel. "Westin and Providence know that Graham and I were friends. So why don't I try talking to one of them and see if I can find out what they're really thinking."

"I'd appreciate that," she told him.

"And if anything occurs to you…if you remember anything Graham ever said or…well, if you happen to have a flash of inspiration about who might have killed him, give me a shout. I mean, you'd obviously tell the guys in charge of the case, but I'd like to be sure they take it seriously. If there's anything I can do to help get that shooter, I want to.''

He took a business card from his pocket, jotted something on it, then handed it to her, saying, ''I put my home number on that. So call if you think of anything that might be significant—no matter how minor it seems. Or if you need something, or just feel like talking. Whatever, okay? And if I don't see you before the funeral…''

''The funeral,'' she murmured. ''I haven't even heard when it's going to be.''

''That won't have been decided yet. The forensic guys have to…''

He didn't finish the sentence, but he didn't need to. He'd said enough. They were talking about a murder victim, which meant the funeral arrangements would be on hold until the coroner released Graham's body.

ANNE AND CHASE WAITED in silence while Rachel saw Dave Hustis to the front door.

Once they'd heard her say goodbye and the door clicked closed, Chase said, ''What do you think?''

She wished she had some brilliant insight to offer, but since she didn't she simply told him she wanted to ask his sister a few questions.

''Let me ask you one first,'' Rachel said, reappearing in the family room. ''When Dave was talking about the Homicide detectives 'almost never' charging the wrong person, how do you think he was defining 'almost never'? More in terms of one in a thousand or one in a million?''

''I don't know,'' Anne admitted. ''It's true that they're careful, though. Unless they've got a confession, they won't press charges without a really solid case.''

''But a solid case *could* be one with only circumstantial evidence, couldn't it? Like the kind that's pointing to me.''

''Rachel, I can understand how you must be feeling, but everything's going to turn out okay.'' Anne forced a smile, wishing she could be certain that what she was saying was true.

''Let's talk about Dave for a minute, though,'' she continued. ''Tell me about him.''

''There's nothing much to tell. I've seen him maybe half a dozen times before—at parties, that sort of thing. The last time was at a barbecue, about a month ago.''

''And why do you think he came by?''

''I'm not certain. I guess Chase told you what his first thought was? That Dave could be the dirty cop?''

''Yes, but what do you think?''

''Well, if he is, I'm sure Graham didn't realize he was into anything. And it's never occurred to me that he might be. In fact, I've always kind of liked him. And I think he likes me.''

She hesitated, then added, ''Actually, I think he *seriously* likes me. I guess maybe it sounds awful to say, but *my* first thought when he showed up at the door was that…''

''Jeez,'' Chase muttered, as Rachel shot Anne a ''you know'' kind of look. ''I thought he was Graham's friend.''

''Rachel *had* broken up with Graham before he was killed,'' Anne quietly reminded him.

''But you don't think,'' she asked, focusing on Rachel again, ''that Dave might have been here on a fishing expedition? I mean, maybe he's honestly concerned about you, but I'm not sure I liked the way he wanted you to tell *him* if you remember anything significant. It's not his case. And did he ask anything before I got here? About what happened at the park? Or what the detectives concentrated on when they questioned you?''

''No, he was basically just commiserating with me—said he knew how awful I must be feeling.''

Anne slowly shook her head. ''I'm not sure whether his offering to talk to one of those homicide detectives was a good or bad thing. What if he wants to learn what they've found out for his own purposes?

''If that's it, he gave himself a perfect excuse to snoop around. Now, if anybody calls him on it, he can tell them he promised you he'd try to get a read on things.''

''What about the private investigator bit?'' Chase said. ''Why did he raise that? Especially when he ended up saying it would just be a waste of money.''

''Well, maybe it was his way of finding out

whether you've hired someone. If he *is* the dirty cop, he'd want to know if there's anyone aside from the police digging around.''

''And I'm sure he'd rather there wasn't,'' Chase said. ''Which would explain why he tried to discourage us on the idea.''

''Wait a second,'' Rachel said. ''Anne, a minute ago you were saying 'if' he's the dirty cop. Now you're both sounding like you're sure he is.''

''You're right. We're getting carried away. So let's talk about something else. Chase told you my father's going to help? That, hopefully, he'll have something for us today?''

Rachel nodded. ''But what should *I* be doing? I mean, this is *my* problem, yet it's you and Chase—and now your father—doing all the work. I feel as if—''

''You could hardly have done anything yesterday,'' Chase interrupted. ''You could barely stand up. And now...'' He paused and glanced at Anne, obviously wanting to hear what she thought.

''But I know most of Graham's friends,'' Rachel persisted. ''What if I talk to them? Obviously, if someone was out to get Graham, Dave wasn't aware of it. But maybe one of Graham's other friends was.''

''Well...'' Anne thought rapidly, her father's warning front and center in her mind.

If there really was a dirty cop, it wasn't necessarily Dave Hustis. It could be just about anyone on the force. And she sure didn't want Rachel saying the wrong thing to the wrong person.

"That's not a bad idea," she finally said. "But if any of Graham's friends had something they figured might help they'll have already told Westin and Providence about it. And if those two heard you were going around asking questions, who knows how they'd react. They wouldn't like it, that's for sure.

"So I think the best thing you can do right now is just lie low and help us from the background. Besides, somebody's got to be here for Julie."

"Good point," Chase said. "She's worried about all this, too, and if I'm off checking on things with Anne, it'll be better for her if you're here."

Rachel nodded slowly. "I guess that's true. We don't want her thinking that we're shutting her out, so I should try to give her some extra attention."

"Why don't you take her out for dinner tonight," Chase suggested. "And to a movie after. She'd like that, and it would probably be good for you, too."

"Maybe it would. If I could just stop thinking about Graham and all the rest of it for even a little while…

"But are you sure there's nothing I can do to *really* help?" she asked Anne. "Or, at the very least, shouldn't I call your father and thank him?"

"Not now. Since we're keeping his involvement unofficial, it'll be better if he can say he's never even spoken to you. But I'll thank him for you. And I'll tell him about Dave. Ask if he'll see what he can find out about him. In the meantime, I'm afraid we're in a holding pattern on everything. Until we know what Dad—"

"Daddy?" Julie interrupted, hurrying in from the deck with Becky on her heels. "Mrs. Slater said you wanted me to stay over there until that black car was gone. But now is it okay if we play computer games for a while? We won't make any noise," she added, her glance darting to Rachel.

"That's okay, honey. I'm feeling better. It's an awfully nice day to be sitting in front of a computer, though."

"But there's nothing to do outside."

"And we're bored with everything at my house," Becky added.

Anne looked at Chase and mouthed *Pool?*

You'd make their day, he mouthed back.

"I was just thinking about a swim," she said to them. "How does that sound?"

JULIE CLIMBED OUT of the pool, still trying to decide if she should ask whether things were okay for Rachel now.

Maybe they were, 'cuz Rachel was gonna take her out tonight. Just the two of them. And when she'd called it "a girls' night out," she'd even smiled. It was the first time Julie had seen her smile since they'd heard Graham got killed, so that had to mean something.

But, then, when she'd said she wasn't going to come over for a swim in case being in the sun made her migraine start up again, Julie'd gotten the feeling she just wanted to be by herself. 'Cuz she was still real upset.

Picking up her towel, she looked over to where her dad and Anne were sitting on the patio. If she asked, he'd probably just tell her the same thing again—that everything was going to be fine. So there really wasn't much point in asking.

"We're gonna spread our towels on the grass, 'kay?" she called over. She kind of wanted to sit close enough to them that she could hear what they were talking about, but she kind of didn't. And they wouldn't say anything good if they knew she could hear them, anyway.

"It'll be softer than lying on the concrete," Becky added.

"Sure, wherever you like," Anne told them. "And what about some lemonade? Sound like a good idea?"

"Yeah! Thanks!" Becky said.

"Yeah. Thanks," Julie repeated. "Want me to help you get it?"

"No, I'll do that while you and Becky organize your towels."

"And put on some more sunscreen," her dad said.

Julie picked up the bottle, then they headed over to the grass.

"Anne's *real* nice, isn't she," Becky whispered as they spread their towels.

"Yeah. I guess."

"Huh? I thought you liked her."

Julie shrugged.

"Well, don't you?"

She pretended that unscrewing the sunscreen bottle was taking all her concentration.

"Ju-u-u-lie? Don't you?"

"Yes. I just…I'll tell you later, 'kay?"

"Yeah, okay."

After pouring a bunch of lotion into her hand, she passed the bottle to Becky—then kept an eye on the patio until Anne come back out of the house with the lemonade.

She stopped at the table to say something, and when her dad laughed Julie's tummy felt funny. As if she'd swallowed too much water in the pool.

She did like Anne, but she wasn't sure she liked her dad liking her. At least, not the *way* he seemed to like her. She'd never seen him look at a woman the way he kept looking at her, and it was making Julie very nervous.

What would happen if he started really, really liking her? If he fell in love with her? If he married her and she moved into their house with them? Would Rachel still live there if that happened?

As Anne started over with the lemonade, the word *stepmother* whispered in Julie's ear.

It made her think about Susie Malinsky. Susie had a stepmother who used to be nice. But only until she married Susie's father. After that she got real mean.

So Julie didn't want a stepmother. She wanted to keep living with her dad and Rachel, just like always. Well, just like for as long as she could remember, at least.

Anne reached her and Becky, handed them their

glasses, then said, "My house is still as much of a disaster as it was yesterday, Julie. So your dad's going to help me move some furniture and start getting things in shape. If you two get bored again and feel like unpacking a few cartons, that would be great—but only if you feel like it."

Becky shrugged to say she didn't care either way, so Julie said, "Sure."

Penelope Snow, the girl detective in Anne's books, sometimes learned things she wanted to know by hanging around adults. And if her dad *was* gonna start really, really liking Anne, Julie wanted to know.

CHAPTER EIGHT

WITH RACHEL AND JULIE OFF for their "girls' night out," Chase and Anne were having dinner at her place again. Not pizza this time, though. On top of everything else she had going for her, it turned out she was a great cook.

The food had come from his house, because she hadn't been grocery shopping yet. But aside from his Caesar salad, she'd done most of the work. She'd also put a white linen cloth on the patio table, as well as a fat little candle. Its flame was lazily undulating in the gathering twilight.

All in all, it was...hell, even a guy like him, who wasn't in the habit of referring to anything as "romantic," knew that was the only word for it.

He took his final bite of the chicken she'd cooked in some wonderful sauce, thinking that, just like yesterday, they'd been together almost every minute of the day.

Oh, after they'd exhausted themselves trying to get her place in order, he'd gone home for a shower and to see Julie and Rachel off. But before he'd left, he'd suggested coming back and making dinner with Anne. Because he'd wanted to be here when her father called. And since they were still waiting to hear from him...

Chase didn't bother finishing the thought, aware he was doing a pathetic job of kidding himself. It really couldn't matter less if he was here when Ben Barrett phoned. If he wasn't, Anne would simply fill him in. So why was he *really* here?

That was hardly a tough one to answer. He wanted to be with her as much as she seemed to want to be with him—a fact that on the one hand made him feel so good he could hardly believe it, and on the other scared the hell out of him.

In the years since Yvonne had taken off for L.A., he'd never been seriously involved with a woman. Casually, no strings attached, yes. Seriously, no. Of course, in all that time he'd never met anyone like Anne.

He still hadn't figured out precisely how or why, but from the very first moment he'd felt so drawn to her, so comfortable with her...

He mentally shook his head, reminding himself that she'd left her husband just as Yvonne had left him. Which would make her a bad bet for a long-term relationship.

Not that he was looking for one. But you sometimes found things you weren't looking for. Like a woman who made your blood run hot and started a tickling in your groin every time she walked into view.

She was beautiful and desirable. And he didn't

think he'd ever met anyone he enjoyed being around more.

However, after making one major mistake in the romance department he sure as hell didn't intend to make a second. Still, if he kept spending every waking minute with her, he didn't know how long he could keep playing this game of see but don't touch. Which meant that what he should do right now was say good-night and head for home.

Just as he was about to, his phone rang.

"You take it," he said. "It's bound to be your father."

She answered—then nodded that, yes, it was.

He waited on the edge of his seat while she and Ben talked. She mostly listened, so he didn't even try to fill in the blanks. Finally, she told Ben about Dave Hustis's visit and asked if he'd see who knew what about the guy.

"I'm not sure what we'll do now," she said after a few seconds of silence. "Let me talk to Chase and I'll call you back. Either later tonight or in the morning. And thanks a million," she added before clicking off.

"Well?"

"He got us more than I was hoping for."

"Great."

"First of all, there was no wallet on Graham's body. But that's not proof of a mugging gone wrong. The murderer might have taken it even if he was there specifically to kill Graham—so the police couldn't rule out robbery as a possible motive."

Chase nodded.

"There wasn't a disk, either."

"Which means the killer took it, too?"

"If Graham had it on him, that must be what happened."

"And Rachel was sure he would have."

"Right. At any rate, as far as Dad could learn, Westin and Providence have no idea that Graham was keeping notes about his case on a disk. So he says Rachel has to turn hers over to them."

"Do you agree with that?"

"Absolutely. Given that his murder might be linked to the case, they've got to have his information about it. It could help them find the real killer."

"'Them,'" Chase repeated uncertainly. "Are you saying that you and I are quitting?"

"No, not necessarily. You printed out all the files, so we've got the information if we need it. But if Westin and Providence follow up on those names Graham recorded... Of course, the problem is they might not. They might only take a look at what's on the disk, then give it to whoever's in charge of the counterfeiting task force."

Something in Anne's expression said that was exactly what she suspected was going to happen, which started an uneasy feeling slithering down Chase's spine.

"You don't think they *will* follow up on the names, do you," he said.

"I...let me tell you the rest of what my father learned. There was no sign of any struggle. And whoever killed Graham was standing several feet away from him when the shot was fired, so it definitely didn't happen the way your caller claimed.''

"Thank heavens." The uneasy feeling had vanished and relief was sweeping through him. "Then there's just no way that Westin and Providence can *really* believe Rachel's guilty.

"Isn't that right?" he said, pressing when Anne didn't immediately agree. "Unless there was a struggle, she couldn't have gotten hold of Graham's gun, so…

"What's the problem?" he asked, the way she was gnawing on her lower lip warning him that his sense of relief had been premature.

"Westin and Providence *do* believe Rachel's guilty.''

"What?"

She gave him an unhappy shrug. "And you were right. I don't think they'll do anything with those names on the disk, because they figure they already know who their killer is."

"But…that's insane. How can they be so damned sure when they're wrong?''

Anne hesitated, wanting to choose her words carefully. Her worst fear about how all of this would eventually turn out was nagging at her again—more persistently than ever this time, because her father's digging had only heightened his concern that she was playing on the wrong team, that Rachel had actually killed Graham.

She forced herself to meet Chase's gaze, knowing

how hearing the rest of the details would make him feel. Yet she couldn't *not* tell him.

"It turned out that one of my father's buddies has been doing some legwork on the case," she began. "When a cop gets killed, a lot of off-duty officers volunteer their time to help out, and... Well, the *how* doesn't really matter. The point is that Dad managed to get a pretty good picture of how Westin and Providence are putting together their case against Rachel."

Chase didn't say a word, simply nodded that she should continue.

"Okay, first, they've got the fact that she admitted being at the murder scene. And admitted she and Graham were arguing. Going from there, they're postulating that she was so angry her emotions were completely out of control."

"What? How do they get to that?" Chase said, his expression tight.

"Because he pushed her hard enough that she fell. And—"

"She said it was more that she slipped than he pushed very hard."

"Chase...*I'm* not claiming he pushed hard. I'm only telling you how their theory goes."

As he nodded again, she couldn't help thinking that when he initially told her the story he'd used the word *infuriated.* He'd said Rachel was so infuriated she didn't say another word to Graham. She just picked herself up, marched back to her car and drove home. But what if...

No, she simply wouldn't let herself go down that road. She'd decided to help the Nicholsons and she was sticking with her decision. And the end result would *not* be Chase hating her because they uncovered evidence that Rachel had pulled the trigger.

"Okay," he said. "According to their theory he pushed her hard, which made her irrational. And then?"

"Well, then they add in the fact Graham was killed by a single bullet to the heart, which, despite what you see on TV, is unusual—unless the killer is a good shot. And Rachel is. They established that by talking to people who've seen her at the shooting range."

"Terrific," Chase muttered.

"Then there's her getting rid of those damned clothes, which they're convinced were bloodstained. And—"

"But it's *all* circumstantial! Do they have *anything* that isn't?"

"Nothing Dad heard about."

"That's because there *isn't* anything! And if there was no struggle, how the hell do they explain her supposedly getting her hands on Graham's gun?"

"Their theory is that he gave it to her. Just before she shot him."

"What! Are they nuts?"

"Chase, calm down."

He stared across the table at her, then shook his head. "Sorry, I'm just finding this totally absurd."

"Do you want me to finish?"

"Yes. Of course."

"All right. They figure that, in the heat of the argument, maybe after he pushed her, Graham drew his gun—either because he was so damned angry at Rachel or just to scare her. Then...well, they don't know *any* of this for sure, but they're assuming she told him how badly he was frightening her, and that brought him to his senses. So he handed her the gun to show her he'd simply overreacted, to prove he really meant her no harm. But after he did..."

"They can't *seriously* believe that. Or expect anyone else to. Can they?"

She hesitated again.

"Can they?" Chase repeated. "What did your father say about that?"

"He said..." She took a moment, then made herself go on. "He said that a good prosecutor might make a reasonable case of it."

"But..." Chase shook his head, as if he were at a complete loss for words.

"Look," she said. "None of this means they'll definitely lay charges. Dad doesn't know if they figure they've got enough to, but his guess is that they'll hold off—at least for a while. That they'll be concerned about proceeding when they don't have the murder weapon."

"Which our friendly extortionist has. Which he'll use against Rachel as soon as he decides I'm not really going to come up with that money."

"Chase, I know this seems bad, but things aren't entirely negative. Don't forget that nobody's sure

Graham was shot with his own gun. Maybe whoever killed him took it from his body after the fact.

"I mean, all they're *sure* of is that he was killed with a Glock. And if it turns out it was somebody else's, then the idea of his handing his gun to Rachel and her shooting him becomes utter fantasy."

"But what if it *was* his? And my caller follows through on his threat and... Dammit, Anne, this is exactly why she's scared half to death. And if we tell her about this crazy theory... You don't think we should, do you?"

"No. She already knows they suspect her. There's no sense telling her things are even worse than she thinks. So if she asks whether they found signs of a struggle let's just say Dad's still checking—that all he knows at this point is there was no wallet and no disk. Otherwise, we'll end up having to explain things we don't want to."

"Okay. But aside from that, where the hell do we go from here?"

"When Rachel gets home," she said, thinking as she spoke, "we tell her she has to call Westin or Providence. That she's got to explain she was keeping a disk for Graham, and why. And she'll say it just occurred to her that whatever he was working on might be somehow related to his murder."

"And then?"

Oh, Lord, how she wished she had a good answer for that.

"Then we'll have to wait and see if they take that possibility seriously" was the best she could come

up with. "See whether they follow up on it or not.
Because if they do, you and I can't. Not without the
risk of jeopardizing a police investigation."

"But your dad will be able to find out? Whether
they actually start investigating that angle?"

She forced a smile. "He's one of the best in the
business, remember?"

CHASE REALIZED HE'D been giving Julie less attention than usual for the past few days, so even though
it was well past her bedtime he sat on the edge of
her bed while she told him about her "girls' night
out."

When she finally wound down and looked as if
she was going to be asleep in three seconds flat, he
kissed her good-night, then headed back downstairs
to where Rachel and Anne were waiting.

"I filled Rachel in while you were gone," Anne
told him before he even reached the foot of the stairs.
"And she'll phone one of the detectives first thing
in the morning."

"Good."

"It's almost eleven," she added, glancing at her
watch. "So I'm going home. But do you want me to
be here when you make the call?" she asked Rachel.
"That recorder my dad lent Chase has a speaker-
phone function. If you use his office phone, we'd
only have to flick a switch and I could listen to both
sides of the conversation—just in case something unexpected comes up while you're talking."

"I'd really appreciate that," Rachel told her.

"When those guys were here, they had me so scared I didn't know how I should answer half their questions."

"Okay, then what if I come over a little before nine? We'd better not make it too early. If they aren't on duty, we don't want to put whichever one we call in a bad mood."

"That's for sure. I'd—"

The sound of the office phone ringing drifted downstairs, stopping Rachel midsentence.

"The extortionist," Chase said, his heart slamming against his ribs.

Turning on his heel, he started rapidly back up the stairs, swearing under his breath. He'd been counting on the guy not phoning again until Monday. But who else would be calling on that line at this time of night?

As he reached the office doorway, Rachel and Anne right behind him, Anne said, "Switch on the speaker function."

He flicked the switch, then took a deep breath, picked up and said hello.

The caller didn't bother with preliminaries. His voice electronically altered, the same as it had been the first time, he opened with, "I said I'd give you a couple of days and you've had them. So you got my money?"

"Not yet, but I'm working on it."

"I said two days."

"Well, that turned out to be impossible."

"Too bad for your sister."

"Look," he snapped, telling himself not to panic. "The only serious asset I've got is my house. So the only way I can raise that much money is by mortgaging it. And you can't get a mortgage in two days."

"No? How long does it take?"

"I'm not sure. But I talked to the manager of my trust company first thing Friday, so he's working on it. He has to arrange for an appraiser to come through, though. And after he submits his report there's all the paperwork and—"

"How long?"

He took another deep breath. "The manager said at least ten working days."

After a second of silence his caller said, "Do you think I'm an idiot? There's no way I'm giving you that long."

"Look, I'll call again on Monday and try my damnedest to hurry things up. But they've got their systems and their rules. And for that big a mortgage they have to get head-office approval. So if you want the money, you'll have to wait."

Chase barely breathed during the silence that followed. If the guy could tell he was lying, they'd just run out of time.

"You better convince them you need that money a lot faster that their rules allow for. Or else figure out some other way to get it. I'll phone you on Monday and see where we're at."

"Dammit, I can't get it by Monday! There's absolutely no way."

"You got a cell phone?"

He glanced at Anne. She nodded.

"Yes."

"What's the number?"

After he rattled it off, the man said, "I'll call on your cellular next time. So you make sure you got it with you every minute. And do your best to have good news for me. Your very best. 'Cuz your sister's not gonna like it if I tell the cops where to find that gun. Not when it'll prove she's a killer. And I don't have a *trace* of doubt it will."

He began to laugh after that, as if he'd just said something hilarious. The electronic altering made the sound positively maniacal—a cross between a hyena's laugh and the scraping of fingernails on a chalkboard. Then the line went dead.

Setting down the receiver, his hand trembling slightly, Chase turned toward the women.

"You handled that perfectly," Anne said. "You couldn't have done better."

"But what happens on Monday?" Rachel asked, her face pale. "What happens when you tell him you still don't have the money and he plants the gun someplace?"

"He won't do that," Anne said firmly. "When he calls back, Chase will stall him again."

Chase couldn't help wondering if she was actually as confident of that as she sounded. He sure as hell wasn't.

"He *knows* it's impossible to get the money by Monday," she was adding. "He's just—"

"But what if he doesn't? Or what if he—"

"Rachel, listen to me," Anne interrupted. "You've got to keep remembering that your fingerprints aren't on the gun, which is a major plus. And now we have him on tape, threatening to plant it, so—"

"That's not quite the way he put it this time," Chase pointed out. He realized he might get Rachel even more upset, yet he couldn't let Anne start deluding herself. They needed her seeing all the facts with perfect clarity.

"He talked about planting it the first time," he continued. "But all he said just now was that he'd tell the cops where to find it. If they listen to the tape, that's not going to give them the same impression as the words *plant it* would."

"And he said it would prove I'm a killer," Rachel whispered.

Chase raked his fingers through his hair, feeling almost certain they'd made a strategic error.

"Look," he finally said to Rachel. "I've started thinking we should have told the cops about this guy right off the bat. So maybe we should come clean now. Give them the tape, explain why we didn't say anything earlier, and tell them exactly what he said on Thursday."

When Rachel glanced at Anne, he added, "That's what she tried to convince us to do in the first place, remember? And her father said the same thing. Right?" He turned to Anne for confirmation; she didn't meet his gaze.

"Yes," she said slowly. "Only...I'd like to hear what he said again. Let's listen to the tape."

He hit the rewind button, then pressed Play once the whirring stopped.

"Well?" he asked after they'd finished listening.

"I'm not sure," Anne murmured. "I know what I told you before, but now I'm thinking we should hold off on telling the police about him."

"Why?"

"Just a gut feeling."

He was about to press her on that when he noticed the way she was eyeing him—and realized she was silently telling him not to continue this in front of his sister.

"I vote with Anne," Rachel was saying. "I'm still convinced he'll know if you talk to the cops. And remember what he said about having a whole bag of tricks up his sleeve? Well, I've got a gut feeling, too. And it's saying those detectives are very close to charging me. So close that even a tiny little trick would be enough to make them do it."

He nodded slowly, telling himself to just drop the discussion for the moment. Because the sooner he got Anne alone, the sooner he'd find out why she'd changed her way of thinking. "I'll walk you over to your place," he told her.

"Change the tape first, so there's no way we can lose that conversation. Put in the spare my dad gave you."

As he did that, Anne tried to reassure Rachel. He could tell it wasn't doing any good, though.

"Okay, let's go," he said, stashing the recorded tape in the top drawer of his desk.

"I'll see you in the morning," Anne said, giving Rachel a hug. "And do your best not to worry."

"I will," Rachel told her. But as they started away she looked both frightened and miserable.

They walked down the stairs and out of the house in silence. Then, as they started for Anne's, Chase said, "What didn't you want to say in front of Rachel?"

"That warning lights started flashing in my head while I was listening to that guy. Did you notice how he emphasized the word *trace?* When he said he didn't have a *trace* of a doubt the gun would prove Rachel's a killer?"

"Uh-huh."

"Well, I think he was taunting you—hinting that if he ends up giving the gun to the cops there'll be some sort of trace evidence on it. Something that would prove she handled it."

"But she *didn't!*"

"No, sorry, I meant there'll be something that will *seem* to prove she did. That's why I changed my mind about wanting you to report his calls. Because if I'm guessing right about what he's up to, and he *does* have some way of learning you blew the whistle on him, Rachel could *really* be up the creek."

Thinking this mess just kept getting more and more complicated, he said, "What sort of trace evidence are you talking about?"

Anne shook her head. "It could be any number of

things. If he got his hands on Rachel's hairbrush, a hair from it would give him a sample of her DNA. Then, by snagging the hair on the gun, he'd make it seem obvious that she'd handled it—fingerprints or no fingerprints.

"Or he could use some sort of fiber evidence. She said her shorts ripped when she fell in the park. So there might have been a bit of fabric or some thread on the ground. The cops would have bagged that, but if our guy picked up a thread before they even got there…well, same thing. He'd snag it on the gun and it would match what the police took from the crime scene. Or if he had a carpet fiber from the trunk of her car…"

"They'd assume she stashed the gun there after the shooting."

Anne nodded.

Chase opened the gate into her yard, quietly swearing. "You really think our guy's smart enough to pull off something like that?"

"I don't know. But maybe this fits together with Rachel's dirty-cop theory. Any cop who's been trained in crime-scene investigation would know all about trace evidence."

"You figure Dave Hustis falls into that category?"

"I doubt there's a police detective who doesn't."

"Dammit. Then his whole purpose in coming by the house could have been to pick up some evidence."

"You're right. But would he have had a chance to

poke around? Or was someone with him the whole time he was there?''

"He'd have had a couple of minutes when I dragged Rachel off to tell her why you were coming over. And she keeps a hairbrush in the main-floor bathroom. So if that's what he was there for, I handed him his opportunity on a platter—without even thinking about it.

"Chase, you can't think of everything. Nobody can. And we don't know for sure he's our guy. He's only a possibility.''

"But dammit,'' he muttered again. "Regardless of who it is, if your theory's right and the cops get that gun, they'll be downright positive that Rachel's guilty. So will a jury. Hell, this is making me wonder if I really *should* try to come up with the two hundred thousand.''

Anne shook her head. "You know that's not the answer.''

He realized she was right, of course. But he also knew what could happen to his sister if he didn't pay up.

"Do we tell Rachel about this?'' he asked as they reached the back of Anne's house.

She turned to him, looking uncertain, then shook her head again. "I don't think that would be a good idea—no better than telling her those detectives are definitely convinced she's guilty. Either thing would only make her more upset. And since she already knows Dave could be her dirty cop, she'll be careful about talking to him next time. If there is a next time."

"Yeah, you're right."

He waited while Anne dug her key from her pocket, trying to convince himself that he didn't desperately want to take her in his arms. But it was like trying to convince himself the sun wouldn't rise in the morning.

He wasn't the kind of man who liked to admit to needing anything. Right this minute, though, he needed to hold someone he cared about. And he cared about her. His feelings for her might have developed awfully fast, but that didn't mean they weren't real.

She stuck the key in the lock, then turned toward him again.

Anne in the moonlight. So desirable she was impossible to resist.

Almost impossible, he corrected himself.

It had to be almost, because if he took her in his arms, how would he ever make himself let her go? And he'd have to. Unless he got home soon, Rachel would worry herself into another migraine.

"You'll manage to stall him when he calls on Monday," she said. "I'm sure you will."

"You really think so? Your father said I probably wouldn't be able to manage it twice."

"Normally, that would be true. But I got the sense this guy didn't give you much time so he could leave himself room to negotiate. That doesn't happen often."

"No?"

"No, so I think we've actually got beyond Monday. And if the cops don't follow up on those names from Graham's disk, you and I will."

"You're assuming your father's going to find out what the cops are doing."

"He will. He can find almost anything once he puts his mind to it."

He nodded, thinking her plan was far less matter-of-fact than she was making it sound. He hadn't forgotten a single word her father had said. Checking out members of a counterfeiting ring wouldn't be a picnic in the park. It would be damned dangerous. And it would take time, too.

"Chase, don't forget that guy is hoping to make a really big score. Two hundred thousand is a lot of money. And he knows that if he gives the gun to the cops, he's also giving up any chance of his big payday. Which means that as long as you can keep him believing you're really in the process of getting the money…"

She paused, then finally just said, "Well, let's not worry about that yet. So…I'll see you in the morning."

"Right."

He tried to make himself start for home, but couldn't. And Anne didn't turn back toward the door. She simply stood looking at him for a long moment, then reached up and gently touched his jaw with her fingertips.

That was all it took to undo him.

CHAPTER NINE

JUST AS IT HAD IN HER DREAM, Anne's hand reached up to touch Chase as if it had a mind of its own.

But this wasn't a dream. And there wasn't even a wisp of mist for him to vanish into. The night was clear, the sky overfilled with stars, her yard awash with moonlight.

He stood motionless while she traced his jaw with her fingertips. Then, just as she was asking herself what on earth had possessed her, he cupped her chin with his hand and leaned closer.

Her heart quickened at his touch. She held her breath as he softly kissed her forehead, her nose, each corner of her mouth. Then his lips met hers and her heart began to race.

His mouth felt as perfect as she'd imagined it would. Warm and gentle, yet decidedly masculine. His scent reminded her of a sultry ocean breeze on a hot Caribbean night, and he tasted of the cognac they'd had while waiting for Rachel and Julie to arrive home. A darkly rich, slightly smoky taste.

The thought that she was at risk of getting drunk on his kiss skittered across her mind. Then he draped his arms around her waist—pulling her closer, deepening their kiss.

The feel of his hard, muscular body sent heat swirling through her. It settled between her legs, and suddenly there was nothing in the world except here and now, her and Chase.

She cradled the back of his neck with her hands, tangled his hair around her fingers and explored his mouth the same ravenous way he was exploring hers. The kiss started her blood pounding in her head, while sweet surges of need began melting her entire body.

His hands slid to her hips, fitting her to him more intimately. He was hard with wanting her; the fresh rush of desire that swept her made her wet with wanting him. Instinctively, she began moving against him, seeking relief from the throbbing ache inside her but only making it stronger—and making him groan.

"Oh, Anne," he finally murmured, ending the kiss and looking down at her.

There was a question in his eyes. But as desperately as she wanted to answer it by inviting him inside, some tattered remnant of common sense warned her not to. So she simply rested her cheek against the solid warmth of his chest and stood in the circle of his embrace, her body heat mingling with his, the rapid beat of his heart synchronized with hers. It made her feel...

When she tried to call up the words, she discovered there weren't any to express exactly how she felt. But it was as if she'd never before been truly kissed. And now that she had been her world was spinning crazily out of control.

"I wasn't planning that," he whispered against the top of her head.

"I started it," she whispered back.

"So...it wasn't a mistake, then."

She didn't know whether he was making a statement or asking a question. But his words stopped the world spinning and brought reality hurrying back— the reality that she might end up pointing the finger of guilt at his sister.

"Or was it?" he said, drawing away a few inches and gazing at her once more.

Was it? If doing something you'd specifically intended not to do was a mistake, then yes, it was. But how could anything wrong feel so right?

"No, it wasn't a mistake," she said at last. "It's just..."

"Just what?"

Forcing herself to step backward, completely out of his arms, she shook her head. "It's just the timing. And the insanity of all this. I only moved here three days ago. And the way we met...the entire situation is so weird that..."

"That we don't want to make it even weirder?"

"Yes. Yes, that's exactly what I'm trying to say."

It wasn't what she *wanted* to say. In fact, she didn't want to say anything at all. She wanted nothing but to kiss him again. Kiss him and far more. Yet now that she was back to staring reality in the face she realized she'd said the sane and sensible thing. And that realization made her press on.

"We shouldn't be rushing headlong into... I normally take this sort of thing very slowly. I don't mean there've been many of...this sort of thing in my life, but... And being neighbors adds an extra complication.''

"Right." Chase jammed his hands into his pockets. "You're right. With everything else that's going on we can't put this in proper perspective. So we should get things sorted out with Rachel. Give the dust from that time to settle. Then see where we are.''

"Yes. That's what we should do. Put this on hold until we see."

"Okay. Then that's what we'll do."

The decision made, he just stood looking at her, apparently no more able to think of what to say next than she was.

Finally, something so obvious came to her that she decided her brain must have been short-circuiting. ''You'd better get back home. Before Rachel worries herself to death.''

"Yes. I'd better. So...I'll see you in the morning.''

She nodded. "About nine."

He half turned away, then turned back. "Get a good night's sleep.''

"You, too," she said, certain that neither of them would get a single wink.

FOR THE HUNDREDTH TIME, Chase forced his eyes back to the plans unrolled on the worktable before him. They'd be completed with only a little more detailing, and he'd hoped to get them finished this morning.

But even though he'd been up well before seven and it was now almost nine, he doubted he'd done more than ten minutes of real work. If he wasn't checking the clock to see how much longer it would be before Anne arrived, he was glancing out the window, hoping to catch sight of her sitting on her patio with a morning coffee, the way he had yesterday.

"You've become downright obsessed with her," he muttered.

Oh, terrific. Now she had him talking to himself. The next thing he knew he'd be... Hell, he didn't know *what* he'd be doing next. All he knew was that he should never have kissed her last night. Because ever since, he'd hardly been able to think about anything except kissing her again. And about how soft and warm she felt in his arms. And about how good she smelled—like wildflowers and love.

"Dammit, *love* doesn't smell," he said, forcing his eyes back to the plans yet again.

Two seconds later, he was glancing at the clock once more.

"Daddy?" Julie said from the doorway.

He looked over. "Uh-huh?"

"Are we gonna work on the model today?"

"I'm not sure. Rachel has to call one of those detectives in a few minutes. And Anne's coming over to be with her while she does. So we'll have to wait and see what happens after that."

"How come Rachel has to call one of the detectives?"

"Because she thought of something that might help them figure out who really killed Graham, so she wants to tell them about it."

"And after she does, everything's gonna be okay?"

"It might not get us all the way to okay, but we should be closer."

"Oh. But how come Anne has to be here?"

"Well…just to give Rachel moral support, really."

"Can't you and me give her moral support? Like always?"

"You and *I*," he said automatically. "And she'll be glad we're around, too. But because Anne was a detective, she's had more experience talking to the police. So we'll make ourselves scarce and let Rachel and Anne handle the call," he added, thinking he didn't really need to listen in on the speaker. Ben Barrett's machine was set to record all the calls on his office line, so he could hear the tape later if he liked.

Julie considered what he'd said for a minute, then wandered into the room, plunked herself down on a chair and gazed at him. "Anne was over here when Rachel and me…when Rachel and *I,* got home last night."

He nodded, a faintly unsettled feeling in his chest. This wasn't the ideal time for a heart-to-heart about what was going on between Anne and him.

"And you were at her house all day. And the day before. And you went back there after Rachel and I went out yesterday, right?"

"Uh-huh, you know I did. I told you we were going to have dinner together."

"So..."

"What's the problem, baby?"

"Well, I was just wondering. After the police don't suspect Rachel anymore, are you still gonna be spending all your time with Anne?"

All his time. Dammit, how often had he told himself that in the unlikely event he ever started to get serious about a woman, he'd take things very slowly? So that Julie had time to get used to the idea and wouldn't feel threatened.

He loved her as much as it was possible for any man to love his child, and he'd never intentionally do anything that would make her unhappy. But she sure didn't look happy right now. She looked frightened.

"Baby, you like Anne, don't you?" he said slowly.

She shrugged.

He swore to himself again. "I had the impression you did."

"She's okay."

That wasn't exactly the response he'd been hoping for, but it was better than her saying she *didn't* like her.

"And she's trying to help Rachel," he said, pressing on. "Which means she has to spend time with us."

"But it doesn't mean you had to move her furniture and stuff, does it?"

Oh, hell, surely he could do better than this. "Julie…she's helping us, so I wanted to do something that would help her. But to answer your question, no, after the police don't suspect Rachel anymore I *won't* be spending all my time with Anne."

"But some of it?"

"Possibly."

"How much?"

"Baby, I just have no way of being sure yet. But I spend time with a lot of other people. You know that. And you also know who's at the very top of my list of people I like being with."

"Me?" she said, giving him a smile that practically made him sag with relief.

"Of course you. Julie, don't ever worry that I won't have enough time for you, because that'll never, never happen."

"Promise?"

"Promise."

"Chase?" Rachel called from downstairs. "Anne's on her way over."

His first impulse was to race down the stairs and take her in his arms, but he reined it in and simply called back, "Good," then looked at Julie again.

"Know what?" he said.

"What?"

"I've got a sudden craving for chocolate ice

cream, so why don't we go raid the freezer while Rachel and Anne make their phone call.''

"I thought the rule was no ice cream before lunchtime."

"Well, we'll amend the rule. No ice cream before lunchtime except when your father gets a craving."

She shot him a grin and they headed out of his office. By the time they reached the family room, Rachel had let Anne in.

"'Morning," he greeted her, trying to sound casual while the mere sight of her started his heart racing.

She was wearing white shorts that emphasized her tan, and a brown T-shirt the exact color of her eyes. She looked positively delectable.

"'Morning," she said, her smile extending to Julie.

He searched her face for a hint that she was having the same absurd reaction to seeing him again as he was to seeing her. There wasn't one. She was a picture of calm, cool and collected. As if nothing at all had happened between them last night.

Swallowing uneasily, he wondered if he'd read more into their kiss than he should have. But he certainly hadn't imagined her passion. Or the longing in her eyes. So she must simply be doing what they'd agreed to—putting what was happening between them on hold for the moment.

But how was she managing to do such a damned good job of it when merely watching her stand there had him all hot and bothered? He didn't know. She obviously hadn't changed her mind about how she wanted to play things, though, so he'd do his best to follow suit.

"Well, I guess we should go make that call," she said to his sister.

Rachel nodded reluctantly. "You're coming up with us, Chase?"

"No, Julie and I have something to do down here."

"How come you're not gonna use the kitchen phone?" Julie asked.

"They want some privacy," Chase told her. "So I said they should use my office line."

As the two women started up the stairs, he followed them with his gaze. Well, he followed *one* of them with his gaze. And watching Anne's cute little behind, in those cute little shorts, made him more hot and bothered yet.

CHASE SAT AT THE KITCHEN TABLE with Julie, thinking about the conversation they'd had upstairs. Whether she wanted to admit it or not, he knew that she figured Anne was more than just "okay."

And Anne was a natural with kids. So if they ended up in a long-term relationship, things would work out all right on that front.

He swallowed another spoonful of ice cream, letting his mind turn to the part that wasn't so good. The fact that Anne had divorced her husband.

Even though, rationally, he could understand why she'd made the decision she had—and even though

he knew that his experience with Yvonne had left
him oversensitive about that sort of thing—it still
bothered him. A lot.

He looked across at his daughter. He didn't want
her growing used to Anne being part of their life and
then... So maybe he'd been right in the first place.
Getting involved with her could prove to be a very
big mistake. On the other hand...

Dammit, half his brain was telling him one thing
and half was telling him something entirely different.
His body sure wasn't giving him mixed messages,
though. All he had to do was glance at Anne's perfect breasts or her shapely little behind to feel a stir-
ring of arousal. And—

The phone began ringing, interrupting his
thoughts.

"Hi, Chase, it's Helen," his next-door neighbor
said when he answered. "Joe and I just decided to
head up to Canada's Wonderland for the day, and
we'd love Julie to come along. Otherwise, he'll have
to go on the rides with Becky, and he's not too crazy
about some of them."

Glancing at his daughter again, Chase wondered if
he shouldn't keep her here and do something with
her. It might be a good idea when she was upset
about all the time he'd been spending with Anne.

Deciding that if she seemed even the least bit re-
luctant about going he'd suggest an alternative, he
said, "It's Mrs. Slater. She wants to know if you'd
like to go to Canada's Wonderland with them."

"Today?"

"Uh-huh."

"Sure!"

"You're positive?"

"Daddy, I *love* Canada's Wonderland. You know that."

"She says she'd love to," he told Helen. "When are you leaving?"

"Oh, tell her to come over as soon as she's ready and we'll go then."

As he relayed the message, Julie gobbled down her last bit of ice cream, then said, "Do you think I need to change?"

"No, but I think you need to wash the ice cream off your face. And here," he added, reaching for his wallet as she pushed away from the table. "Tell the Slaters I want to buy them a beer. And some lemonade for you and Becky."

She stashed the bills in her pocket, made a mad dash for the main-floor bathroom and emerged three minutes later with a clean face.

"Is it okay if I go without saying 'bye to Rachel? And Anne?"

"Sure. I'll say goodbye for you. And have a good day, huh?"

"I will." She gave him a big hug, then raced out the front door and over to the Slaters'.

He watched until she disappeared into their house before locking the door and striding rapidly up the stairs.

"Perfect timing to miss everything," Anne said

teasingly. "Rachel just finished talking to Detective Providence two seconds ago."

"And?"

"He'll be by in an hour or so to pick up the disk."

"Did he sound as if he figured it might give them a lead?"

"He sounded…" Anne glanced at Rachel. "Would you say 'noncommittal' about sums it up?"

Rachel nodded. "He was polite enough. And he said he was glad I'd called and they'd have a close look at what's on it. But…" She shrugged. "I guess I was hoping for more."

"Well," Anne said, "I'll phone my father right now and tell him Providence is coming to get the disk. And I'm sure he'll be able to learn whether they actually follow up on those names or not, so we'll just have to sit tight until he does."

"Sit tight?" Rachel murmured uneasily. "But tomorrow's Monday. And when that guy calls again—"

"Rachel, I don't like the sense that we'll be doing nothing, either," Anne said. "But as I said last night, when he calls again Chase will buy us more time. I'm positive he'll be able to. And it shouldn't take long for my father to find out what we need to know.

"Until then… We really don't have a choice, it's as simple as that. Without more information, we might do something stupid and screw up."

Do something stupid and get ourselves killed, Chase knew she meant.

Glancing at Rachel, he decided she wasn't at all

convinced that "wait and see" was the best plan, so he tried to think of something reassuring to say. Before he could, there was a knock on the front door.

"Julie was heading up to Canada's Wonderland with the Slaters," he said, starting for the stairs. "She must have forgotten something."

"Go ahead and call your dad," Rachel told Anne. "I'll just run down with Chase and say goodbye to her."

Rachel right behind him, Chase reached the door and pulled it open. Instead of Julie, Detective Dave Hustis was standing on the front steps.

He gave Chase a nod, then looked past him at Rachel. "This isn't a bad time, is it?"

"No, not at all," she said.

When Chase didn't move out of the doorway, she subtly poked him. He stepped backward, wondering what the hell Hustis wanted this time. Hadn't he managed to get his trace evidence to frame her with yesterday?

Reminding himself they weren't sure there even *was* a crooked cop involved in all this, let alone that it was Dave, he followed along into the living room. Regardless of what they were sure of, he didn't intend to let the guy out of his sight.

Rachel gestured their visitor toward one of the love seats, then sat on the one across the coffee table from it. Chase sank down beside her, pretending not to notice that Dave's expression was saying he'd rather just talk with Rachel.

"I came by," he said, "to let you know that Graham's funeral is set for Tuesday morning."

Chase took Rachel's hand and gave it a squeeze as Dave told them the time and place. They'd be there, of course, but it would be hard on her.

"I was wondering," Dave continued to Rachel, "if you'd like me to take you."

"I'll be going with her," Chase said.

Yesterday, she'd mentioned that she'd always kind of liked Dave. So he didn't know just how seriously she was taking the possibility that the guy was her dirty cop—especially since they hadn't filled her in on Anne's hypothesis about the trace evidence. Chase, however, was taking the possibility damned seriously.

"Chase? Rachel?" Anne called from the back of the house.

"In the living room," he said. "We're talking to Dave Hustis," he added, so she wouldn't say anything she shouldn't before she realized Dave was here.

"Oh…hi again," she greeted him, pausing in the doorway.

"Hi," he said. Then he looked at Rachel once more. "The reason I asked about the funeral is I thought it might be a good idea for you to attend with a police detective. For appearances' sake, I mean. And on top of being a cop, I was Graham's friend. So your being with me would imply…well, if I believed you had anything to do with his death, I'd hardly be there with you."

Rachel glanced uncertainly at Chase, then said, "Maybe the three of us could go together."

"Sure," Dave said. "Sure, that's a good idea."

Good wasn't the word Chase would have chosen, but now that Rachel had suggested a threesome he'd have to go along with it. Besides, he knew Dave was right about the appearances angle, so he simply let the subject drop and asked if Dave had gotten a chance to talk to Westin or Providence yet.

The instant the question was out, he wished he could take it back. What if Dave said the same thing Anne's father had? That the detectives were certain Rachel was guilty. It was the last thing she needed to hear.

Fortunately, it wasn't what Dave told them.

"I left a couple of messages," he said, "but I haven't heard back yet. I'll let you know when I do."

He pushed himself up from the love seat and added to Rachel, "In the meantime, as I said yesterday, if there's anything I can do for you or anything you want to talk about, just call me."

While Anne waited in the living room, Chase trailed along to the door, said goodbye to Dave, then hovered in the hall while the guy talked a little more with Rachel—trying to figure out what he was really up to.

Good cop or cop gone bad? Law-abiding citizen or extortionist? Graham's friend or Graham's killer?

The instant the door clicked closed, Anne appeared in the hall.

"What do you think?" he asked her.

"I don't know," she said, shaking her head. "Coming here once to console Rachel, I'll buy, but coming again the very next day?"

"He wanted to tell me about the funeral," Rachel said.

"He's got a phone," Chase pointed out.

She shot him an annoyed look, then glanced at Anne and said, "You know, I really hesitate to say this, because I'm so grateful for everything you're both doing for me. But I think you're totally wrong about Dave. I'm sure he just feels very badly about Graham's death, and he knows I'm feeling even worse. So he's trying to be kind. That's all there is to it."

"Maybe you're right," Anne murmured.

"Yeah, maybe," Chase agreed, following her lead. But he wasn't convinced.

CHAPTER TEN

RACHEL BEGAN TALKING about the restaurant she'd taken Julie to the night before, so Anne continued to linger over her coffee, half listening, half letting her thoughts drift. Last night, she hadn't told Chase everything her father had said when he called. She'd left out the part where, once again, he'd expressed concern that Rachel might not be telling the whole truth and nothing but.

It made her uneasy, because his gut feelings were usually right. Still, despite that, she kept growing more and more certain that Rachel was innocent. And she had to go with her own feelings, not his, which meant she should simply stop worrying about turning up evidence of Rachel's guilt. Unfortunately, that was easier said than done.

She snuck another glance at Chase and began thinking about a different part of last night—the part when he'd taken her in his arms and kissed her. A warm glow ignited inside her as she recalled how it had made her the happiest woman in the world.

From there, she moved on to thinking that the idea of putting things on hold with him was the stupidest one she'd come up with in her entire life. Or that he'd come up with. She couldn't actually remember whose brainstorm it had been, but it was undoubtedly the dumbest plan she'd ever agreed to.

However, that clearly wasn't the way he felt, because he'd been avoiding her from the moment she'd arrived this morning—hardly easy to manage within the confines of his house, but he'd done his best.

First, he'd been nowhere in sight when she got here. Then he'd stayed downstairs, with Julie, while Rachel phoned Providence. After that, he'd probably have vanished entirely if Dave Hustis hadn't shown up. Obviously, he intended to have as little as possible to do with her until…

Her worst fear about that came slinking back. Maybe he wasn't merely thinking it was a good idea to put things on hold ''until.'' Maybe he'd had second thoughts about getting involved with her at all and ''until'' would turn into ''forever.''

Uneasily licking her lips, she told herself that if he was the sort of man who blew hot and cold from one day to the next she was lucky to have learned it now.

But if that's what he turned out to be, she certainly wouldn't feel lucky. Not by a long shot. Even the possibility it might be true had her far more concerned than she wanted to admit. And sitting here, barely able to keep her eyes off him for two seconds at a stretch, was only making things worse.

She let herself look at him one more time, her gaze resting on his sensual mouth, her thoughts returning to how she'd felt with her body pressed to his. Then she said she had to leave.

"Well, I can't thank you enough for coming over," Rachel told her. "I'm not sure I could have made myself dial Providence's number without you beside me."

"No problem. And as soon as I hear from my dad again we'll decide what we should be doing next."

"And you'll hear from him *very* soon, right?"

"Definitely. He'll do the very best he can for us," she added, thinking that Rachel's anxiety level was so high it must be off the scale.

"I don't like your being without a phone," Chase said as she rose to leave.

She shook her head. "We can't risk my taking your cellular again. You've got to have it in case that guy decides he wants to talk to you before tomorrow."

"You think he might?" Rachel said.

She sounded so nervous that Anne wished she hadn't raised the possibility. "I think it's pretty unlikely," she said. "I just want to be on the safe side. At any rate, my phone's being installed on Tuesday morning. Unless… Rachel, are you sure you don't want me to go to the funeral with you? I could wait another day or two for a phone."

"Thanks, but you didn't even know Graham. And I'll have Chase there."

"And Dave Hustis," he muttered.

"Are you taking Julie?" Anne asked.

"No," he said. "Given the situation, I don't think it would be a good idea."

"Then would you like me to keep an eye on her while you're gone?"

He hesitated a second before saying, "Thanks. I'll ask her if she'd be okay with that. Helen Slater's got Becky enrolled in a couple of summer classes, and she takes her to one of them on Tuesday mornings.

"But getting back to the phone, if you need to use one, just come over. And whenever your father calls I'll be right here. I'm going to arrange things so I'm close to home until we get Rachel's problem solved."

"Great," she said, hoping that "solved" didn't prove to be far-too-optimistic a word.

"I'll walk you down the yard," he added as she rose to go.

She didn't know whether that was good news or bad. Maybe he wanted a minute alone with her to tell her... Lord, she didn't know what he might be intending to tell her and she was afraid to find out.

When she'd bought her house, she'd hardly expected to discover a terrific man living right behind her—let alone imagined herself falling for him. But now she had a horrible feeling that just when she'd met someone she thought might possibly be Mr. Right, his second thoughts had told him she was Ms. Wrong.

"What do you figure?" he said as they started down the deck steps. "Is Dave Hustis our guy?"

So that was what he wanted to discuss. It had nothing to do with them. But why *didn't* he want to talk about them? Why didn't he want to say he was so crazy for her that he'd changed his mind about cooling things between them? That he didn't even want to do it temporarily, because he'd rather be with her every waking minute?

"Anne? What do you think?"

"I just don't know," she said, forcing her mind to Dave. "But my father said he's put out some feelers. So we'll hear what other cops think of him."

"Well, since they were friends, Graham obviously figured he was okay. Although that might only mean he's a good actor."

"It could. Yet Rachel likes him, too. And you said her intuition's good. On the other hand, if there actually *is* a dirty cop... Well, aside from the detectives handling the case, he's the only cop who's put in an appearance."

"Two appearances," Chase reminded her. "You think I should tell Rachel I don't want her being alone with him? Even though she gets annoyed as hell if I tell her what to do?"

"Under the circumstances, I think it would be worth annoying her."

He opened the gate but didn't follow through into her yard. "I'd better head back before Providence comes by for that disk," he said. "Rachel will feel better if I'm there."

"Right," Anne murmured. "And I'll talk to you after I hear from my dad."

He merely nodded, then turned away, leaving her wondering why he hadn't said a single word about last night—and afraid the reason was that he simply wanted to forget about it.

JULIE DABBED A DROP of glue on the bottom of a tiny tree, then carefully placed it on one of the penciled dots. Her father always set his models on a big base, so the client could see how the buildings would look surrounded by landscaping. And he used lots of trees. He said people were happier if they had green space outside their offices.

Satisfied that the tree was stuck solid, she glanced over at him. Last time she'd checked, he was working on his computer. Now he was gazing out the window—in the direction of Anne's house. Where she'd be staying tomorrow morning while he and Rachel went to Graham's funeral.

She'd said that would be all right when he'd asked, but later she'd started worrying that she'd feel funny being alone with Anne. Of course, she hadn't that first day. Anne had been easy to talk to. But that was before…

She glanced at him again. He was still gazing out the window. "Dad?" she said.

"Uh-huh?"

When he turned toward her, she took a deep breath, then asked, "Are you ever gonna get married again?"

He just eyed her for a minute. "I don't know," he said at last. "Do you think I should?"

She shrugged, pretending she'd never really given the matter any thought. If he knew she and Becky had spent half their time at Canada's Wonderland talking about him and Anne, he wouldn't like it.

"What made you ask, baby?"

"Oh…I was just wondering," she said, suddenly worried that this might not be such a good idea after all.

"We've never really discussed it, have we?"

She shook her head.

"So…why don't you tell me what got you wondering about it."

"I don't know," she said, staring at her sandals. If she didn't look at him again, maybe he'd just go back to his work. He didn't, though.

"It wouldn't have anything to do with what we were talking about yesterday, would it?" he asked. "About the amount of time I've been spending with Anne?"

"Well…maybe." She should have known he'd start reading her mind as soon as she opened her mouth.

"But I wasn't with her last night, was I," he said. "I was right here waiting when the Slaters brought you home. And I'm not with her today, either. I'm with you."

"I know, but…"

"Julie, Anne and I haven't known each other nearly long enough to even think about getting married. And if I ever was considering it, with anyone, I'd tell you. Right away."

"But if you *were*… What would happen to Rachel? Would she still live here with us?"

"Baby, we'd work everything out when the time came. Rachel would be fine."

He hadn't said she'd still live here, though.

"And you'd be fine, too. It would all work out."

"You're sure?"

"Sure I'm sure."

"And you'd tell me if you were even thinking about it?"

"Isn't that what I just said?"

She nodded, feeling at least a tiny bit better.

"Why don't we take a lemonade break?" he suggested, pushing back his chair.

"Good idea!"

Chase followed his daughter out of the office and down the stairs, wondering if he'd handled that okay. He hoped so, but it was hard to know with kids.

In any event, it had reminded him that he had more than himself to take into account when it came to Anne. And being a natural with kids didn't necessarily mean she'd want one around day in and day out.

Of course, he really had no idea how she'd feel about that. But it was hardly the sort of topic he could raise with a woman he'd kissed precisely once. So what was he supposed to do? Guess? Or just wait and see if things actually went anywhere between them, then worry about the rest of it?

See *if* things went anywhere? Hell, why didn't he just admit they were bound to? Because the more he thought about it, the more convinced he was that he had a serious once-burned, twice-shy hang-up. And he was damned if he was going to let a hang-up make him do something as stupid as backing off from Anne Barrett.

ANNE SAT STARING at her computer screen, trying to decide how Penelope Snow should figure out who was stealing bikes from the neighborhood.

Between worrying about how many hours were slipping away while she waited to hear back from her father and wondering how things really stood between her and Chase, she was having a tough time concentrating. But if she didn't try to work, she'd only spend more time worrying and wondering—which would be totally unproductive. So what was going to happen in the damned plot?

Would it be best if Penelope uncovered a clue? Tried surveillance? Or maybe setting up a sting would be a good idea. If one of the kids had a brand-new bike that would make perfect bait...

"Damn," she muttered as yet another image of Chase crept into her mind and derailed her train of thought.

Yesterday, after she'd come home from his place, she'd spent the rest of the morning setting up her "real" computer in the bedroom she'd chosen to make her office. She hadn't wanted to write outside on her laptop—where glancing over at his house was only too easy to do.

But her out-of-sight, out-of-mind plan hadn't worked. No matter how hard she tried to concentrate on what she was doing, the next thing she knew she was thinking about him again. And the problem had just gotten worse since he'd wandered over this morning.

He'd only wanted to check that her offer to look after Julie tomorrow was still good. But the instant she'd seen him her heart had started skipping beats and her palms had begun to sweat.

When the mere sight of him did that to her, there was no point in trying to deny that she'd fallen for him. Had he fallen for her, though?

The other night, she'd felt sure he had. And she still wasn't entirely ruling it out. Maybe that was only wishful thinking, but she kept telling herself he might merely be steering clear of her because he thought that's what she really wanted. After all, putting things on hold *was* what they'd agreed to.

But what if that wasn't the explanation? He'd said he hadn't planned to kiss her. So what if it had only been the magic of the moonlight that had made him do it? And then, come the next day, he'd realized that he didn't really feel anything—

Before she got further along that track, she heard someone knocking downstairs. On the *back* door.

She raced down the stairs and, sure enough, it was him. Her heart began to pound—even before he held up his cellular and she realized her dad must have called for her.

"No word from our extortionist?" she whispered, taking the phone.

"Not yet. But I've been jumping every time the damn thing rings." He took a backward step, adding,

"I left Julie up to her ears in glue, so I've got to go help her put things away. Come over as soon as you're finished?"

She nodded, then let her eyes linger on him as he turned away and she said hello to her father.

"I don't have much that's new," he told her. "Only a couple of things. First, as far as I can gather, Dave Hustis is one of the good guys. And he definitely wasn't the shooter. He was working at his desk, surrounded by half a dozen other detectives, at the time of the murder."

"Well, I'm glad to know that. But when we've been speculating all along that two people might be involved in this, it doesn't put him entirely in the clear, does it."

"Uh-uh. He could still be your crooked cop. Assuming there really is one. After all, if a dirty cop's smart, the only people who know he's not one of the good guys are the bad guys."

"Right." So Dave was still a *maybe*.

"What about the names on the disk?" she asked. "Do Westin and Providence figure there's even a chance that someone in the counterfeiting ring killed Graham?"

"Anne, they're still convinced it was Rachel. And from what you told me, nothing in his files indicated he was concerned about his life being in danger, either from a ring member or anyone else. So—"

"Then what was the point of having Rachel give them the disk? I thought it was because you figure Graham's death is related to the case."

"Assuming it wasn't Rachel who killed him."

"Dad, I really do think that's a safe assumption. The better I get to know her... Well, I just think you can trust my judgment on this."

"You're probably right," he said—slowly enough that Anne wasn't sure how convinced he was.

"But to answer your question," he continued, "part of the point in having her give them the disk was to make her look as if she's trying to help. Which will be important if she ends up on trial."

Anne firmly told herself things wouldn't come to that. Not if she did her job well enough.

"Plus, I was hoping one of those guys might spot something in Graham's notes. Something that didn't mean anything to you but was actually significant."

She closed her eyes, unable to stop herself from wondering exactly how he'd meant that.

Was he saying that Westin and Providence had access to information she didn't? So they might have spotted something that couldn't *possibly* have meant anything to her? Or had he been hoping they'd pick up on something important that she'd simply failed to notice?

Telling herself not to go there, she said, "Then the bottom line is that they don't intend to check out the names. Is that it?"

"I can't be certain. But I'm guessing they won't. Aside from anything else, the counterfeiting task force is still in the midst of its investigation.

"If a couple of police detectives started questioning ring members about Graham's murder, it would probably blow that operation out of the water. So they're not likely to risk screwing it up when nothing on the disk reached out and grabbed them.''

"No. No, I guess they aren't.''

When her father remained silent, she said, "Well...listen, I *really* appreciate your help. And if any of your buddies hear anything more—''

"Wait a minute. Let's discuss where you're going from here. Are you still thinking about nosing around after those people yourself?''

"One of them might be the killer,'' she reminded him.

"That hardly answers my question. Are you still thinking about nosing around after them?''

"Dad...what else can I do?''

"You can quit while you're ahead, darling. This isn't something I'd have wanted you tackling when you worked with me. And it sure as hell isn't something I want you tackling now. You've got to be rusty, Anne.''

She closed her eyes again, knowing he was right but not wanting to admit it. Not even to herself.

"I promised I'd try to help,'' she said. "I—''

"And you *have* tried. But there are limits.''

Limits to what he believed she *should* do or what he believed she *could* do?

There was another, longer silence. Then he said, "All right, if you're that determined at least let me help. I'd feel a hundred times better if you weren't getting into something like this alone.''

"I wouldn't be alone. Chase would be helping me."

"He's a complete amateur. I'm not. Anne, fax me Graham's notes on those twelve ring members and you won't believe what I'll be able to come up with—and it'll take almost no time. In just the few years you've been gone from the field, the Internet's revolutionized it. Some of the databases I can access now are phenomenal."

She hesitated, knowing deep down that what she really wanted was to be good enough to ID the killer on her own. With only a complete amateur's help. She wanted the chance to prove to herself that she could do it. And prove it to her father, as well, she silently conceded.

But she wasn't at all confident she'd be successful on her own. She didn't have the resources or experience her father had, and time was in short supply— even if Chase did manage to stall the extortionist again. And if she failed, where would it leave Rachel?

She considered that question, then forced herself to say, "I saw how many files were on your desk the other night. Are you sure you can spare the time to help?"

CHASE, ANNE AND RACHEL sat on the deck, Anne speaking quietly because Julie and Becky were in the backyard, playing a lawn-toss game.

Chase was leaning forward in his chair so he wouldn't miss anything, which put him close enough

to Anne that the heavenly scent of her perfume and
the sight of her even more heavenly legs were wreak-
ing havoc with his concentration. Each different pair
of shorts he saw her wearing seemed to make her
legs look more sensational.

When she finally finished recounting the conversation she'd had with her father, he glanced at his
sister. Her face was pale and drawn.

"Rachel...try to relax, huh?"

After she'd given him a wan smile, he turned to
Anne again. "Where do we go from here?" he
asked, even though he thought he knew—more or
less.

She'd told him that if the cops weren't going to
follow up on those names, they would. But she
hadn't explained exactly how they'd do it. Or how
they could possibly get to all of them before the extortionist grew tired of waiting.

"Well, whether Dave's part of this or not," she
said, "at least now we're sure he didn't pull the trigger. So we want to establish if any of those men
Graham named could have. In other words, try to
establish where each of them was last Wednesday
evening. And the ones we can't do that for become
our prime suspects."

"How fast can we do that?" Chase glanced anxiously at his cellular, sitting on the drinks table beside him.

It was almost five, but most trust companies, including his, stayed open till eight or nine. If the ex-

tortionist thought about that, he might wait until later to phone.

Even if he did, though, a few extra hours were nothing. And if the next conversation didn't go well, they wouldn't have time to establish where a single one of those people had been last Wednesday.

Telling himself to lose the negative thoughts, he forced his attention to Rachel.

"But what about Westin and Providence's suspects?" she was saying, her voice quavering a little. "Do they have a single one aside from me? Or are they so convinced I killed Graham that..." She stopped midsentence and shook her head.

"I don't really know any more details," Anne said gently. "There was a limit to how much my dad could find out."

Chase looked at her once more, thinking she'd neatly avoided telling Rachel that those detectives were totally convinced she'd killed Graham. Which was just as well. Rachel was close to falling apart, and they still had the funeral to get through.

"They're going to arrest me, aren't they?" she murmured.

"Rachel, no," Anne said. "I've been saving the good news for last. From here on in, my father will be actively working with us."

Relief whispered in Chase's ear. Thus far, nothing they'd done had involved any real danger. But that wouldn't be the case if they started asking around about a bunch of criminals. So having Ben Barrett actively playing on their team would be a godsend.

"We're going to fax him what's in Graham's notes about the ring members," Anne continued. "I saw a fax machine in your office, didn't I?" she added to Chase.

He nodded.

"Well, he said he can access some databases that store tons of personal information about people. So he'll get what more there is on those names, then he'll follow up on half of them while you and I take the other half. And once we've narrowed the list down to people we can't establish alibis for…" She shrugged. "We'll get to that later. Right now, let's go send him what he needs."

"How soon do you think you'll hear back from him?" Rachel asked.

"Knowing him, he'll get on the Internet the minute he's got those notes. And he said I'd be amazed at how fast he'd have results. We might even be able to do something useful tonight, depending on what he comes up with."

"I'll be here with Julie," Rachel said quickly. "If you want to go anywhere, I mean."

"We'll have to see what he finds," Anne told her. "But if there's anything we can start on immediately, we should."

Chase nodded, glad she was thinking that way. He could practically feel the extortionist breathing down his neck.

"There's some lasagna in the freezer," Rachel said. "Why don't I go stick it in the oven. Then, if you *can* get started tonight…"

"That's a good idea," Anne said.

"Why don't you invite Becky for dinner," Chase suggested. "If she's here, it'll keep Julie from worrying about what we're up to."

As Rachel started down off the deck to talk to the girls, he picked up his cell phone, then ushered Anne into the house—wondering how many people would have put as much effort into helping them as she had.

Not many, he knew that much. And they were nowhere near done yet. Anne was...dammit, she was absolutely fantastic. There was no better phrase to describe her.

He headed up the stairs after her, watching her cute little behind again, and silently amended his thought. There were phrases like "sexy as hell," "positively gorgeous" and several more of that ilk. But if "absolutely fantastic" wasn't right up at the top of the list, it was close.

They'd just reached the upstairs hall when his cellular gave a quick double ring and his heart froze for a moment. The official workday had ended at five. This wasn't likely a business call.

Anne whirled around, then stood stock-still as he answered, "Chase Nicholson."

"You got my money?" the mechanically altered voice asked.

He nodded to Anne, silently telling her it was the call, then he ordered his pulse to stop racing and said, "Not quite yet, but I spent the day doing my damnedest to speed things up."

"And?"

"And the appraiser's coming tomorrow."

"What time?"

For half a second he drew a blank. Then his mind began working again. The funeral was in the morning. This guy undoubtedly knew that. "He said early afternoon. And once he's been, my guy's going to bust his butt to push the mortgage approval through."

"So you'll have the money when? By the end of tomorrow?"

"No, they just can't do it that fast. I thought I told you, the appraiser has to write a report and—"

"I'm running out of patience!"

"I know. But, dammit, I'm doing everything I can."

"Everything doesn't seem to be enough."

"I'll get it. That's not the issue. The issue is—"

"If not tomorrow, then when? Wednesday?"

"They won't say for sure. They said as fast as they can. That's the best I could get out of them."

"And you figured that'd be good enough to save your sister's ass?"

"Look, I realize I can't *make* you wait. If you decide to give the cops that gun there's nothing I can do to stop you. But if you do, you don't get the money. So it's your decision."

Chase listened to the pounding of his heart during the long silence that followed.

"I'll think about it," his caller said at last. Then he hung up.

"Where are we?" Anne demanded as he clicked off.

"I don't know." Quickly, he recounted the other side of the conversation.

"I think you did it," she told him. "We'll have to find someone to show up tomorrow afternoon and play appraiser—in case he decides to watch the house. But I think you bought us at least a little more time."

His relief was tempered by anxiety. "A little more time" might not be nearly enough. And there was no guarantee he'd actually bought them even that.

"How do we know for sure?" he said. "I mean, what if he does give the damned gun to the cops? He might even do it tonight."

"We'll know if he does. My dad will hear right away. I have no idea what sort of favor he called in, but he said we'd know."

"Okay. That's great. At least there's one thing we don't have to worry about."

When she gave him a forced smile, he managed one in return, although it wasn't easy. Not when there were still a zillion things they *did* have to worry about.

"What?" she said softly. "What are you thinking?"

He simply shook his head. He could hear Julie and Becky starting up the stairs, so this wasn't the time to tell her he was thinking about taking her in his arms and holding her forever.

CHAPTER ELEVEN

AFTER DINNER, CHASE AND ANNE retired to his office, leaving Rachel, Julie and Becky watching TV.

First, he phoned a buddy and explained that he needed a favor, that someone had to show up at the house tomorrow afternoon looking like an appraiser.

"You mean you want me measuring and making notes?" his friend asked.

"Only while you're outside. When you come in, you can have coffee with Rachel."

"Change that to a beer and you're on."

"You've got it. And thanks, Ray."

"No problem."

Once that call was finished, the two of them waited for Anne's father to phone.

The minutes ticked by in slow motion. They were both so anxious he could feel the tension in the air. What if Ben hadn't managed to learn anything more about those men Graham had named?

Reminding himself that Anne had seemed certain he would, he reached for her hand and gave it a squeeze—as much to reassure himself as her.

She squeezed back, which was more than enough to start him thinking about taking her in his arms again. But this definitely wasn't the time or the place, so he simply sat wishing it was.

Finally, a little after seven o'clock, Ben called.

"Okay, I've got information on six of the ring members," he told Chase. "I'll fax it to you, then see what I can dig up on my half of the names."

That was the good news. The better news came after he filled Ben in on the extortionist's latest call.

He said he figured Anne was right—that Chase had actually managed to buy them more time. Still, the question remained how much more.

When he asked it, there was a pause before Ben said, "There's no way of telling. He could phone you back tonight. But if we're lucky, it'll be a couple of days."

"And what do I do when he does?"

"You'll have to play it by ear. Anne won't be able to listen in now that he's phoning on your cellular, so you're the one who'll have to judge whether you can bluff him again."

"What if I get the feeling I can't? That he won't go for another delay?"

"Then tell him you've practically got the money. Say it'll be waiting at the trust company for you in the morning. Or, if he calls in the morning, tell him they said you can pick it up just before closing. What we need you to do is get us a few more hours without making him think you're actually trying to stall him."

"A few more hours to…?"

"To figure out what the hell we do next. Assuming

we haven't established who the real killer is by then.''

"I see," Chase said, his stomach churning. If the best they could hope for was another day or two, that assumption was probably a good one.

But what if he tried to buy more time and failed?

The police would get the damned murder weapon, with something linking it to Rachel, that was what.

And if he didn't try, if he said he'd have the money when he really wouldn't... What if he did that, and then they weren't able to figure out what the hell to do next?

"I'll start faxing this stuff as soon as we hang up," Ben told him. "And remind Anne she's going to keep me informed."

"Right. Thanks, Ben."

He'd barely passed the message on to Anne before his fax machine began receiving.

She grabbed the first page as it finished, quickly read it, then handed it to him.

It contained data about a thirty-six-year-old man named Andy Crocker, and the amount of detail was incredible. He'd realized the Internet was gobbling up people's privacy, but he'd never imagined so much personal information was available to anyone with access to the right databases.

Andy Crocker had a long list of prior addresses, including the Don Jail and the Kingston Penitentiary. His present occupation was variously referred to as "handyman," "casual laborer" and "courier."

The second man, however, had no police record.

He was an insurance executive with a wife and children. He drove a Mercedes, owned a thirty-foot sailboat and had season tickets to both the Maple Leafs and the Blue Jays.

"What's a guy like this doing in a counterfeiting ring?" he asked.

Anne glanced up from what she was reading. "Remember what Graham's notes said about the controlling members? They lead seemingly normal lives. That's the best cover for any criminal. If you've got a good life-style but no apparent source of income, people get suspicious fast.

"This one's a long-haul trucker," she added, looking back at the sheet in her hand. "Which has to be the perfect occupation. He probably distributes fake cards to runners all over the country. Maybe transports some of the things they purchase with them, too."

One by one, they went through the pages.

Two of the men were controlling members of the ring—Ken Bentley, the insurance executive, and a man named Harry Cochrane, who owned a collision-repair business. The other four were lower-level members.

By the time Chase had finished reading Ben's data, he knew more about each of them than he did about most of the people who lived on his own street. He was just going to say that when Rachel appeared.

"What's happening?" she asked, looking as if she expected the worst.

Glad they had better than that to tell her, he said, "Anne's dad sent us a ton of information."

"So it's enough to help?"

Anne nodded. "Now it's just a matter of figuring out where to begin. And we might as well start with Gary Hooper, the trucker," she added to Chase. "His sheet says he lives alone, which means fewer potential complications. Let's see if he's home."

As she reached for the phone, Rachel said, "I'm feeling awfully restless. I think I'll take the girls out for ice cream or something."

"We might not be here when you get back," Anne said.

"That's okay. I'm going to go to bed when Julie does. I haven't been sleeping well, and tomorrow will be a rough day."

After Rachel headed back downstairs, Anne checked the sheet on Hooper and punched in his phone number. She listened briefly, then clicked off, saying, "He's not home and there's no answering machine."

"We start with one of the others, then?"

She shook her head. "Uh-uh, let's stick with him. Actually, his being out is good. Assuming he's still not home when we get there, we'll see what we can learn from his neighbors. That's often really productive.

"I'll just take these over to my place," she added, gathering up the pages. "And change into a dress. I'll only be a few minutes."

Barely a quarter of an hour later, they were on

Highway 401, heading east through the northern part of the city. Thirty minutes after that, Chase exited at Warden Avenue and made his way to Cornwallis Drive. Beside him, Anne was trying Hooper's number again—on the cellular this time.

"Still no answer," she said as he pulled up in front of the man's house. "And there's a neighbor sitting on the porch next door. This is perfect."

"But there's a car in the driveway. Maybe he just isn't answering his phone."

"His car would be there if he's off on a haul. But I'll go see what's what," she added, getting out of the Cherokee.

Chase resisted the urge to climb out after her and follow along up the sidewalk.

During the drive over, she'd given him a mini-course on how to investigate people, so he knew she'd rather work this particular trick alone. But, dammit, Hooper might come to the door. And any one of the men on their list could be a killer.

Telling himself she knew what she was doing, he simply sat where he was. But that didn't keep his heart from thudding or his adrenaline from pumping. He sure as hell could see why her father had been concerned about her getting into this. If anything awful happened to her...

He shook his head, not wanting to even think about how he'd feel if something did. He might only have met her a few days ago, but he was beginning to believe she was meant for him, that fate had decided he'd been on his own for long enough and nudged her into buying the Kitchners' house.

She rang the bell. He started to sweat.

Then she rang it again and he felt a little less anxious. Hooper didn't seem to be in there—which meant that now she'd wander over to the neighbor's and tell him she was an out-of-town relative, trying to get in touch with Hooper while she was visiting Toronto.

Finally, she turned and started back down the front steps, glancing around uncertainly and then pretending she'd just noticed the man on the porch.

As she walked across the front lawn toward him, her hair shining in the lingering rays of the sun, Chase's heart began beating faster again. Her white dress had a short skirt, and the way it hiked up a little with each step she took was almost making him drool.

She was so damned gorgeous. And look at that smile she was giving the guy! How could he resist telling her whatever he knew about Hooper?

Chase sat watching her talk with the man, feeling as if he was falling harder for her with each passing minute. Was that possible?

It certainly wasn't something that had ever happened to him before. But no one like Anne Barrett had ever walked into his life before.

Finally, she started backing away from the house, gave the neighbor a little wave and headed toward the Jeep.

"Well?" he said, reaching over to push open the door for her.

"One eliminated. Our trucker's doing a haul all the way to Vancouver and back. And he left last Tuesday."

"The day before Graham was killed." Chase started the engine and pulled away from the curb. "The guy's positive it was Tuesday?"

"Uh-huh. His wife lets Hooper's cat out in the morning and in at night when he's away. But she plays bridge on Tuesday nights, so the husband had to do it last week."

Chase nodded, then said, "You know, when Hooper gets back, he'll go crazy trying to figure out who his beautiful long-lost relative was."

"Beautiful?"

He swallowed hard, wishing the word hadn't slipped out. One glance at Anne, though, made him stop wishing.

She was blushing, obviously pleased. And the way she was gazing at him, her dark eyes filled with warmth, made him hot. It also started him thinking they must have come to the same conclusion. Their putting-things-on-hold idea was downright stupid.

With that thought swirling around in his head, he had a hard time resisting the urge to drape his arm around her shoulders and pull her close. But they were almost at the 401, and a sixteen-lane highway was hardly good cuddling territory.

Later, he promised himself.

TWILIGHT WAS FADING to darkness when Anne and
Chase arrived back from their trip to Gary Hooper's.

"Rachel and Julie might have turned in already,"
he said. "So I'll just drop you off at your place."

Anne nodded, trying to decide whether she should
ask him in. She wanted to, but it might be an extremely bad move.

The more time she spent with him, the more she
wanted to spend. Just being with him made her feel
wonderful; it was as simple as that. However, if being with her didn't affect him the same way, then
the further things developed between them, the big-
ger the potential heartache.

He said he thinks you're beautiful, she reminded
herself. The mere recollection was enough to make
her glow inside. But even if he hadn't been exag-
gerating, thinking she was good-looking and feeling
the kind of emotional attraction she felt for him were
two very different things.

Not that she was *only* attracted to him emotionally.
Not at all.

She snuck a peek at his rugged profile and her
pulse stuttered. Then her gaze slipped to his neck,
and the sexy way his hair curled down onto it made
her blood temperature shoot up ten degrees.

Yes, the physical attraction was undeniable. But
there was far more than that. On her side, at least. It
was his side she wasn't sure of.

As he pulled into her driveway, she made her decision. She wasn't going to invite him in, because if
he kissed her again the way he'd kissed her before,

she wouldn't have a rational thought left in her head. Which meant the only smart thing to do was say good-night right here and—

"Would it be okay if I came in for a few minutes?" he asked. "We could take another look at the information your father dug up. I can't help worrying that we'll run out of time, so I'd feel better if we figured out where we're going next."

He gave her a smile that practically melted her, then added, "If *you* figured out where we're going next is what I should have said."

"No, it isn't. I want you to tell me every idea that occurs to you. This sort of thing's hardly an exact science. We can try anything we think might work."

When he turned off the ignition, she realized he'd taken her words as a "yes" to coming inside. Within a split second, her mouth was dry, her palms were wet and her heart was skipping beats. The raw physical reactions made her extremely aware that she hadn't felt this way about a man since...

Lord, she couldn't recall ever feeling this way before. Not even with her ex-husband. There was something about Chase Nicholson that turned her inside out and upside down—a fact that both excited and frightened her.

She knew things had been developing awfully fast. Yet that didn't seem bad. In fact, it was almost magical. As if she'd suddenly been dropped into a fairy-tale world where only good things could happen.

Reminding herself she was still in the real world, whose inhabitants included killers and extortionists, she got out of the Jeep and headed for her front door, Chase so close behind her she was aware of his body heat. That started her heart beating even more erratically.

"Coffee?" she said once they were inside.

"Sounds good."

"Those pages are on the table," she told him as they reached the kitchen. "Why don't you read through them again while you're waiting."

She took the can of coffee from the cupboard, then her gaze found its way over to him and she simply couldn't force it anywhere else. She watched him pull a chair away from the table, angle it toward her, then sit down.

As he stretched his long legs out in front of him, his jeans pulled tightly across the muscles of his thighs. When they did, she couldn't stop herself from imagining his legs entwined with hers.

She wanted to make love with him. Tonight. There, she'd admitted it. But she didn't want to do something she'd come to regret. And she was terrified that by doing the one she'd also be doing the other.

Finally managing to look away from him, she took the top off the can. Her hands were trembling a little, but she spooned the coffee into the maker without spilling any. She did almost as well with the water, creating only a minor pool on the counter.

After flicking the on switch, she got a dishcloth and carefully wiped up the spill, trying to use the time to relax, but not succeeding very well.

"You know," Chase said as the water began to burble, "when I see all these facts, I don't have a clue what to do with them. The further we get into this, the more I realize just how much I need you."

He needed her. Even though she knew he hadn't meant it *that* way, she felt a little weak in the knees.

"Well, if I was designing a building," she told him, scrambling for something to say, "I wouldn't know what to do after the walls were sketched in."

Still feeling incredibly anxious, she got the milk from the fridge, then put it and the sugar on the counter.

"I take mine black," he told her.

"Uh-huh, I remembered that," she lied. She'd had coffee with him before, so she *should* have remembered. But her brain didn't seem to be working quite right.

There was enough coffee made to fill the two mugs, so she did that, adding milk to her own. As she started over to the table with them, Chase rose and scooped up the pages, saying, "Why don't we sit in the living room. That big couch of yours is really comfortable."

She had little choice except to follow him.

The living room, however, was no more fully set up than any other room in the house. At the moment, it had just one lamp in it—and not a very bright one. Which meant the only way they'd both be able to read was by sitting right beside each other on the couch.

Since he'd helped her arrange the room, he knew

that. But had he been thinking about it when he'd made his suggestion or not? Half of her hoped he had. The other half hoped he hadn't.

She mentally shook her head. The way things were going, the man would turn her into a schizophrenic.

He tossed the pages onto the coffee table, then took his mug from her and sank onto the couch. Her pulse doing an erratic little dance, she carefully set her coffee down before joining him.

"Great coffee," he said, taking a sip.

"Thanks."

As he put his mug on the table, she leaned forward to pick up the pages. He caught her hand midreach, his touch so charged it almost made her jump—and left the air between them humming.

"Anne?" he said softly.

She merely looked at him. Whether wanting him was wise or foolish, she wanted him so badly that his dark gaze alone was enough to start her aching for him.

Without saying another word, he moved closer, cradled her head between his hands and kissed her.

It was a hungry kiss that drew the breath from her body and made her chest feel too tight for her heart. A kiss that set fireworks off inside her and started flames licking her belly. A kiss that said she was his woman. His alone. To make love with. To possess.

When he finally drew back, he left her silently begging for more.

"This time, I *was* planning that," he whispered.

"For how long?" she whispered back.

"I'm not sure. But I was planning on doing it more than once."

"Good plan."

Smiling one of his bone-melting smiles, he reached up and turned off the light, leaving only the moon shadows drifting in through the front window to see by.

He wrapped his arms around her; she rested her hands on either side of his face and softly pressed her lips to his, tracing them with her tongue.

"Oh, jeez," he whispered, his breath hot against her mouth.

She tangled her fingers in his hair, and as her tongue began dancing with his some of her nervousness slipped away—hand in hand with most of her doubts. She still didn't know how it had happened so quickly, under such strange circumstances, but this man had become incredibly special to her.

Kissing her greedily, he eased her down on the couch beside him. When his hands found her breasts she moaned with longing and the tight, desperate ache between her legs made her press her lower body to his. Feeling the hardness of his erection only excited her more.

"Chase," she murmured, slipping her hands beneath his T-shirt and up his back. His skin was so warm and enticing that even her palms began to tingle with desire.

He found the zipper on her dress and tugged it down, his lips never leaving hers, the heat of his body setting her afire. How could she have ever thought this would be a bad idea?

For a moment, he hesitated, saying, "Anne, are you sure?"

When she nodded, he rose, taking a condom package from his pocket and ripping it open before he tossed it onto the coffee table.

Quickly, he stripped off his clothes. A second later he was bending over to help her undress. Then he simply stood gazing at her.

She suddenly felt…exposed. Vulnerable. What if he didn't—"

"You are *so* gorgeous," he said, cuddling down beside her again.

She breathed a sigh of relief. "I'm also *so* nervous," she admitted.

He brushed her hair back from her face. "Then you're not entirely sure. I…Anne, I know we said we'd wait and see, but…you must be able to tell how I feel."

"How do you feel?" she whispered, her gaze not leaving his.

"I think you're wonderful. I think…" He paused, slowly running his fingers along her jaw. "Anne, I think I've fallen in love with you."

He loved her! For an instant, her heart stopped beating and the world stopped turning. Then her blood began dancing in her veins and she felt as if she was about to start laughing and crying at the same time.

Somehow, she managed not to, and simply murmured, "Oh, Chase, I think I've fallen in love with you, too."

He smiled such an infectious smile that nothing in the universe could have stopped her from smiling back.

"And I didn't mean I wasn't entirely sure," she told him. "It's only that…it's been an awfully long time. I don't do this with just anyone."

"I know you don't. And I don't do it with just anyone, either."

Lowering his head, he softly kissed his way down her throat. They were hot, wet little kisses that did crazy things to her insides.

"Do you have any idea how heavenly you smell?" he whispered. "Or how heavenly you taste?" he added, his mouth reaching her breasts.

She tried to say that he smelled and tasted heavenly, too, but her breathing was suddenly so rapid and shallow she could only moan in reply.

Swept away. That was what was happening— Chase was completely sweeping her away. She couldn't think, could only feel. Couldn't speak, could only whimper her pleasure.

The urgent throbbing between her legs had her moving her hips against his body and clutching him even closer to her. She wanted him to devour her, to be part of her, to keep doing what he was doing all night long.

He suckled on one breast and teased the other nipple with his thumb, sending electric darts of fresh desire through her. When he reached down and slowly began caressing his way up her inner thigh, she felt as if she'd die of need.

"Oh, Anne," he said thickly. "How could I have ever thought I'd be able to keep my distance? Even for a little while?"

She licked her lips, but still couldn't speak. His erection was hard against her belly now, and every remaining shred of her awareness was focused on that. Reaching for his hips, she tried to guide him into her.

"Wait," he murmured.

She froze, the terrifying thought that he wanted to stop shooting through her brain. But he was only grabbing the condom and putting it on. Then he kissed her stomach and gently slid his finger into her.

She knew she was outrageously wet but didn't care—didn't care about anything in the world except having him inside her.

When he entered her, she moaned with the ecstasy of it. When he began to thrust, she cried out. And when she came, tears were streaming down her face.

He thrust a final time then collapsed onto his side and lay against her, breathing raggedly. Finally, he cuddled her to him, making her smile through her tears.

"What's wrong?" he murmured into her hair. "What's wrong? Did I hurt you?"

She shook her head. "Nothing's wrong. I just sometimes cry when I'm really happy. Nothing's wrong at all."

"Good," he whispered, cuddling her closer still.

FOR THE FIRST FEW SECONDS after he opened his eyes to the pale light, Chase thought he'd died and gone to heaven. And heaven was waking with Anne, naked in his arms, her soft curves pressed against him and her hand enfolded in his.

Then reality crept into his still-sleepy brain and reminded him what had happened last night.

They'd made love. Fantastic, glorious love. There was a sheet draped over them, and he had no idea how it had gotten there, but he certainly remembered the important part.

And, obviously, after making love, they'd fallen asleep right here on the couch.

Carefully, trying not to wake her, he shifted his body so he could see her face. She looked as contented as he felt, which started him thinking about waking up with her beside him every morning. What would that be like?

Heaven on earth.

The words tiptoed through his mind, lingering long enough that he had time to decide they might be exactly right.

Gazing at her for another moment, he wondered whether that's what she'd think. Maybe it was too much to hope for, but maybe not.

"Mmm," she murmured, her eyes slowly opening.

She simply looked at him for a second, and then she smiled. He felt as if his heart would burst with happiness.

"'Morning," she whispered.

"'Morning," he said, nuzzling her neck.

"You fell asleep."

"Looks to me as if we both fell asleep."

"Well, you did first. And I wasn't sure whether I should wake you and send you home or not."

"You decided not."

She smiled again. "I decided that if you woke up when I went to get the sheet, it would be an omen."

"Ah."

Reluctantly, he checked his watch. It wasn't even six, and neither Julie nor Rachel was an early riser, but he knew he'd better head home.

"So," he slowly said, caressing her bare shoulder.

"Mmm," she murmured, "that feels good." Then she rested her hand on his thigh and began to draw a circle with her fingertip.

She'd drawn precisely half of it before he was rock-hard and desperate to be inside her.

"You should go home now, shouldn't you," she teased.

He grinned. "Right. I'll just kiss you good-morning, then get going. Unless one thing leads to another," he added before capturing her mouth with his.

CHAPTER TWELVE

JULIE WOKE UP with her heart pounding, so scared it took her a minute to feel certain she was safe in her bedroom—and that the man with the gun had only been in her dream.

Propping herself up, she looked at the clock. It was just a little after six, so normally she'd snuggle back down and fall asleep again. As Rachel always said, Daddy was the only early bird in the Nicholson household.

But what if she went back to sleep and had another bad dream? Besides, she kind of had to go. So maybe she'd better do that, then see what she thought.

After finishing in the bathroom, she walked the rest of the way along the hall to her dad's office. Sometimes, he worked for a while before breakfast. Not today, though.

She started back through the silent house toward her own room, and as she passed Rachel's door she heard a muffled sound. She stopped dead and stood listening for a few seconds before she realized her aunt was crying.

Uh-oh. What should she do? Daddy had warned her Rachel would be really upset today, 'cuz of the funeral. So maybe she should go in and see if she could help. Or maybe she shouldn't. Rachel didn't like people to see her crying.

She glanced toward her father's bedroom—thinking she couldn't just do nothing—then walked over and knocked real quietly.

He didn't answer, but if she knocked any louder Rachel would hear, so she opened the door a crack and whispered, "Daddy?"

Still no response.

Opening it farther, she tried again. When that didn't work, she decided she'd better go in and give him a little poke.

But he wasn't in bed. It was made and there was no sign of him. So where was he?

After hurrying downstairs, she checked the main floor and called to the basement. Now she was getting as scared as that dream had made her.

She looked into the backyard, then ran to the living room window and peered out front. He wasn't there, and his Jeep wasn't, either. Okay, then, he'd gone somewhere. But where would he go so early?

Back in the family room, she stood gazing toward Anne's house, thinking that Penelope Snow, girl detective, would be able to figure this out. So how would she do it?

Well…first she'd see if anything was written in her dad's appointment book.

Julie headed back upstairs and into his office. But there was nothing in his book for so early, and nothing else that seemed like a clue. No piece of paper on his desk with a name or address scribbled on it or anything like that.

"Rats," she whispered. She wouldn't make much of a detective. Not like Penelope Snow.

Of course, it was really Anne who did Penelope's thinking. So maybe, if she stared at Anne's house real hard, she'd get some good detective vibes.

Hopefully, she walked across to the window. As she looked down, she noticed that beyond the roof of Anne's garage she could see part of the driveway. And her father's Jeep was parked in it.

She eyed it for a minute, wondering what he was doing at Anne's already. And why he'd driven over, instead of just going through the back gate.

Then she realized the truth. He'd been with Anne last night. And he hadn't come home.

Her tummy suddenly felt as if it was full of marbles and her throat began to hurt. She didn't want him to be over there. She wanted him to be here. With her and Rachel. Where he belonged.

ANNE AND JULIE SAT on the edge of the pool in shorts and T-shirts, sipping orange juice stacked with ice cubes and dangling their bare feet in the water. *Silently* dangling their bare feet in the water.

Every time they'd been together before today, Julie had been talkative. But not this morning. She'd been answering each question with a nod, a shrug or a monosyllable, and it was making Anne very uncomfortable.

Trying again, she said, "You're sure you don't

feel like a swim? I'll go over with you to get a bathing suit if you'd like.''

When the child merely shook her head, she told herself not to take it personally. Julie had to be upset about Graham's funeral. And because she was still afraid that Rachel would end up in jail. But wouldn't it be a good idea for her to talk about her fears?

Probably it would. She clearly didn't want to talk, though, and Anne wasn't at all certain she wanted to press.

She understood children well enough that she could write books they related to. But with writing you could go back and revise to your heart's content. In real life, you just had a single shot at saying something, and she never exactly brimmed with confidence when it came to dealing with kids one-on-one.

Being an only child, she had no nieces or nephews. So she simply didn't know enough children to have had much practice.

As she gazed over the water, the nagging fear she'd been trying to suppress came wiggling back into her brain.

What if it was more than the funeral and worrying about Rachel that had Julie so quiet? What if part of the reason she wasn't talking was that she'd decided she didn't like her new neighbor?

Exhaling slowly, Anne let her thoughts turn—yet again—to Chase. She'd known from the beginning that any woman who got into a relationship with him would be getting into one with Julie, as well. And if the girl actually *had* decided she disliked her...

Lord, she didn't even want to consider the possibility that might be true. She loved Chase. He loved her. And the more she thought about a future with him the more she wanted it.

Glancing at Julie again, she began thinking about the best way to ask if she'd done anything wrong. She was still trying to come up with the right way to phrase it when the faint sound of her doorbell drifted out to the yard.

"That must be the telephone installer," she said, pushing herself up. "I'll be right back."

It only took a couple of minutes to show the man where she wanted the new jacks, then she left him to do his thing and started back down the stairs.

As she passed the living room doorway, her gaze caught on the couch and warmth rippled through her. Just the recollection of last night made her unbelievably happy. And whatever it took, she was going to ensure that things worked out between her and Chase's daughter.

She retraced her steps across the patio and lowered herself to the edge of the pool. "I'm back."

Julie nodded.

After taking a deep breath, she said, "You're being awfully quiet. Do you want to talk about what's bothering you?"

"Nothing's bothering me."

"Oh. I was thinking you might be feeling bad about Graham."

Julie looked at her then.

"Did you know him very well?"

She shrugged. "Sometimes I saw him when he came to get Rachel. And a few times they took me and Becky places. To the zoo and stuff."

That was better. Three sentences in a row was real progress. "Then I guess you felt pretty sad when he died."

"Yeah."

Keep quiet, Anne told herself. Whether silence was uncomfortable or not, letting it work for her was a trick she'd often used during her investigator days.

The longer it stretched the harder it was to maintain, but finally Julie said, "You know how Rachel was in the park with him? Just before he got killed?"

"Uh-huh?"

"Well, sometimes I think what if it was Rachel who got killed, instead."

"Ah. That's an awfully scary thought, isn't it."

"Yeah. 'Cuz Rachel's almost like my mom. I mean, she does all the mom stuff."

"I've seen that."

"And my dad really likes her living with us. So he's never gonna get married again."

Anne uneasily licked her lips. She doubted that Chase had told Julie he'd never remarry. He was the sort of man who'd be careful what he said when it came to a "you never know" subject like that. But Julie's tone had made it clear that she *hoped* he wouldn't. Was that part of what was bothering her, then?

Likely it was, Anne decided. The chemistry between her and Chase had to be obvious. So if Julie'd picked up on it and that had her worried enough to try to warn off a potential candidate…

Finally, she said, "You know, when I was growing up, I didn't have a mother living with me, either. Mine died when I was only two."

"Really?"

She nodded. "And *my* father never got married again."

"How come?"

"He always says he just didn't meet the right woman."

Julie stared at her feet for a minute, then looked at Anne once more. "If you didn't have a mom, who took care of you?"

"Oh, different people. My dad always made sure there was someone when he was at work, and my grandparents helped out a lot."

"My grandparents live in Peterborough."

"Your father mentioned that."

"And my other ones, my mom's parents, are way out west, so I almost never see them."

"Well, at least Peterborough isn't very far. It's only about ninety miles, right?"

"I guess. But it's far enough that I don't see them all the time. Not like Becky. She sees hers every week.

"Mine phone a lot, though. And now they're phoning every single day, 'cuz of Rachel. After they saw all the stuff on TV, they were even gonna come and stay with us for a few days, but she said no, she'd be okay."

"Ah."

"I wished she'd said yes. It's fun when they come."

"Well…" Anne wasn't sure what else to say, so she just left it at that.

Julie lapsed into silence once more, then finally said, "When you were little, did you want your dad to get married again?"

"That's a hard one, because in a way I did and in a way I didn't. I mean, I used to be afraid he'd decide to marry someone awful. But if he'd fallen in love with a woman I liked, and who liked me, I think it would have been good.

"And now that I'm a grown-up, I wish he had. Because I sometimes worry that he's lonely."

Julie splashed the water with her toes. "My dad won't be lonely even after I grow up, 'cuz he'll still have Rachel."

Anne bit her tongue—and told herself to quit while she at least thought she was ahead.

A SEEMINGLY ENDLESS procession of cars, including Dave Hustis's, slowly followed Graham Lowe's hearse en route to the cemetery.

"There were so many people at the church," Rachel murmured, her voice catching. "And all those officers in uniform. I wasn't expecting that."

Chase leaned forward in the back seat and silently rested his hand on her shoulder. He was pretty choked up himself.

"That's how it usually is when a cop's been murdered,'' Dave was saying. ''Every major police force in the country sends representatives. And Graham had a lot of friends on the Toronto force. Dammit, we've just got to get the bastard who killed him.''

Nobody spoke again for a block or so, then Dave glanced at Rachel and said, ''Would you talk to me about what happened in the park?

''I don't mean right this minute,'' he added before Chase could intervene. ''But soon? There could be something you forgot to tell Westin and Providence. Or something might strike me that didn't strike them. Or—''

''Let her have a chance to think about it,'' Chase told him. Regardless of which side Dave was actually on, the last thing Rachel needed was to be pressured.

She turned and gave him a grateful look—her eyes swimming with tears.

Eventually, they arrived at the cemetery and wound their way through it to their ultimate destination. Once Dave had parked, Chase climbed out and opened the front door for Rachel. She clung to his arm as they walked from the road toward the grave site.

''Let's not go any closer,'' she whispered when they were about halfway. ''I just can't.''

The three of them stayed where they were while the sea of mourners closed in around the minister. When he began to speak, his words barely reached them.

''You see Westin and Providence?'' Dave asked quietly, nodding toward one edge of the crowd. ''See how they're checking people over? If they recognize anyone who, by rights, shouldn't be here, they'll follow up.''

"Someone like…?'' Chase asked.

"Oh, a member of organized crime or a known felon. There really is a morbid fascination that draws some killers to their victim's funeral. It's one of the few things the movies get right.''

Chase stood watching the detectives, thinking they might merely be putting on a show. After all, the other cops would be expecting them to survey the scene. On the other hand, maybe they weren't *entirely* certain that Rachel was their killer.

Hoping to hell that was true, he let his own gaze drift over the mourners—and spotted Ben Barrett. For half a second he wondered why the man was here, then he realized Ben was doing the same thing as Westin and Providence. Scanning the crowd for a killer.

But how would he have any idea who he was looking for? Unless he'd gotten hold of pictures to go with some of those names. Maybe that was it. If he was one of the best in the business, he probably came up with angles that most people would never dream of.

Still, the odds on finding the right face in a crowd couldn't be a lot better than the odds on finding the proverbial needle in a haystack.

The minister had begun to pray, so Chase bowed his head. When the prayer ended and he opened his eyes, tears were streaming down Rachel's face.

"It's over, so let's get out of here," he said, wrapping his arm around her.

"I should speak to Graham's parents," she managed to say. "I'm afraid to, though. What if *they* think I killed him?"

"They don't," he told her, although he had no idea what they thought. "But you're in no shape to talk to anyone."

AFTER ANNE AND JULIE had eaten lunch, they'd gone back to dangling their feet in the pool. And much to Anne's relief, things were going well.

She'd told Julie the basic plot of the book she'd just started, and they were in the midst of figuring out some of the details when Chase opened the gate and came through.

It was the first time she'd seen him in a suit, and she liked what she saw. Of course, every time she looked at him she liked what she saw—regardless of what he was wearing.

Or not wearing, an imaginary voice whispered in her ear.

It would have made her smile if her thoughts hadn't turned to the funeral. "How was it?" she asked quietly.

He merely shrugged, but his expression said it had been tough.

"Is Rachel okay?" Julie asked. "Did she cry?"

"Yeah, she did, baby. She's still sad, but she'll be all right. I need you to come home with me now, though, and keep her company, because Anne and I have some things we've got to do.''

'''Cuz the police still suspect her, right?''

"Julie, I thought you were going to try to stop worrying about that.''

"I *have* been. But I can't.''

He held out his hand to her and looked at Anne again. ''I'll be back after I change, okay?''

"Fine.''

She waited until the gate closed behind them, then retreated to the patio, glad of some time alone to think about her and Chase. And Julie and Rachel.

She'd realized the two of them were close. But when Julie had said, ''Rachel's almost like my mom,'' it had started Anne thinking about some of the ramifications of that fact.

While she'd been growing up, she'd only worried about getting stuck with a stepmother she didn't like. But Julie also had to worry that if Chase married again she'd lose Rachel, who was more of a mother to her than her biological mother.

And that was what *would* happen. If Chase remarried, regardless of who his new wife was, Rachel would probably move out. But while adults would see that as the logical course of events, how would Julie see it?

That wasn't a hard question to answer. She'd blame Rachel's departure on her new stepmother—unless the situation was handled very carefully, with a good deal of discussion beforehand.

Plus, Julie would need long enough to adjust to

the idea before the fact. And to really get to know the woman her father intended to marry.

Glancing over at Chase's house, she told herself she might be getting way ahead of herself. He'd said he loved her; he hadn't said he wanted to marry her. If he did, though...

She shook her head, thinking how many horror stories she'd heard about children bent on causing trouble in relationships. Then she started wondering how she'd have behaved if *her* father had remarried.

From there, it was only a short step to suspecting she was part of the reason he hadn't. Strangely enough, until she'd come face-to-face with Julie's situation, she'd never really thought about that. But now that she was, it seemed likely.

She'd been far from a perfect child, and a downright difficult teenager—definitely not ideal stepdaughter material.

Had that made her father decide he'd be wiser to stay unattached? Was it the reason he was alone now?

She considered the possibility for a bit, then headed into the house. She had her own telephone again and hadn't even used it once. So she'd just give him a call and see what he was up to.

WHEN CHASE ARRIVED BACK at Anne's, she was in the kitchen with a cordless to her ear.

My father, she mouthed.

He stood watching her, thinking that every time he saw her she looked more desirable.

"Well, thanks again," she said after a few seconds. "I'll talk to you later."

As she set the phone on the counter, he draped his arms around her waist and pulled her close. She felt so soft and warm and alive it took his breath away.

Had they really made love for the first time only last night? He knew they had, of course, yet it seemed utterly impossible. She was already such an integral part of his life he could barely believe he hadn't always been in love with her.

He gave her a long, lingering kiss that made him wish he could carry her up to her bedroom right this minute. But he couldn't.

Yesterday, her father had said they'd be lucky if their extortionist didn't call back for a couple of days. And a couple of days only took them to tomorrow. With that in mind, he eased back from her embrace and simply gazed at her.

"That was nice," she murmured.

"Only *nice?*"

She shot him an adorable grin and said, "Would *extremely* nice make you happier?"

"Well, it would certainly be an improvement. But, you know, after this is over and done with I want to spend an entire week just kissing you."

"*Just* kissing me?" she teased. "Nothing more?"

That made him smile. For the first time all day. "W-e-e-ll, maybe we could start with kissing and see where we end up," he said.

She laughed; he felt a rush of pleasure—also the first of the day.

"You know what I think?" she asked.

"No, what?"

"I think we should work on getting this over and done with just as fast as we can."

He smiled again. "Sounds like a plan to me. So what did your dad have to say? Did you know he was going to the funeral?"

"No, he told me he was there, though. And he's started checking on the rest of the names. But what about Dave Hustis? Did you get a better fix on where he's coming from?"

"No. He didn't talk much, although he asked Rachel if—sometime soon—she'd tell him exactly what happened in the park. Said he might pick up on something that Westin and Providence missed."

"That makes me nervous."

"Me, too."

"I know he and Graham were friends, but it's not his investigation. He isn't even Homicide. So why is he trying so hard to stick his nose in?"

"I don't know, but I don't think Rachel should talk to him about it."

"I don't, either. How did he seem during the service? Upset?"

"Yeah. Everyone was, though. It got pretty emotional."

When he didn't go on, Anne softly said, "You okay?"

"Pretty much. Only..." He hesitated, suspecting he shouldn't get into this right now, yet feeling compelled to.

"You know," he continued at last, "aside from the hard time Rachel had, what really got to me was thinking that Graham was a couple of years younger than me. It started my mind going about the whole issue of life being uncertain. Of how you have to reach out and take what you want when you get the chance. Because, otherwise, the chance might pass you by."

He paused, hoping Anne would agree. The mere thought of missing out on the chance to have her made his chest ache.

When she was silent, he shrugged and said, "I guess that sounds corny, but it's true. Seeing Graham lying in a coffin just drove it home to me. He never married, never had kids, probably thought he had all the time in the world for that sort of thing, and it turned out he didn't." He told himself to stop right there, then discovered he couldn't.

"It's like with us," he continued. "If we'd stuck to our putting-things-on-hold idea..."

She gave him a small smile. "It would only have delayed the inevitable."

"Probably. But you never know. Something unexpected might have happened and...you understand what I'm saying?"

"I'm not sure," she murmured.

"I'm saying that we love each other, and...well, I know it's been awfully fast, but it just seems so damn right that I think we should—"

"Chase?"

"What?"

"I do love you. I love you more than I'd have ever believed I could. And it seems right to me, too. But we've got to take things slowly, give the situation a lot of time and thought. Not start shouting our feelings to the world just yet."

A sinking sensation had begun in his stomach and was rapidly spreading through his entire body. Shouting his feelings to the world was precisely what he felt like doing.

"There's Julie to consider," she continued. "And Rachel. We can't just go turning their lives upside down without—"

"Do you think I haven't thought about that? I realize I'll have to talk with them. And that Julie will need a while to adjust. I'm just saying... Oh, hell, I should have left this for another time."

Anne was silent for a moment, then said, "Chase, we're seeing things the same way, you know."

He merely shrugged. If he said anything, it was liable to come out sounding sarcastic as hell.

"We are," she insisted. "We both realize we've got to make sure we get all our ducks in a row. So that everyone's okay with what's happening.

"And you're right about this not being the best time. We have too much else on our minds and too much still to do. Which means we should wait to talk about where we're going and how fast until after...well, you know."

"Yeah, I know," he forced himself say. "I guess the funeral got to me more than I realized. Started me thinking... But you're right. There's no real reason to rush into anything. So let's get back to those names. Have you had any other ideas for following up?''

For a moment he didn't think she was going to let him switch subjects just yet. But she finally said, ''Actually, yes, a couple of them. One I just thought of while I was talking to my father. It only involves a phone call, but it might do the trick.''

''Good,'' he said, although he'd barely heard her words. He'd been too busy listening to his mental replay of what she'd said before.

There's Julie to consider. That phrase had really grabbed him, because it was so important to him that they *did* consider her. But it had also reminded him of something he'd been thinking of yesterday—that he had no idea how Anne would feel about suddenly having a child around day in and day out.

Was that part of the reason she'd looked so uneasy when he'd started talking about the future? Did she need time to decide whether she wanted to take on a man with a daughter?

Hell, it shouldn't be much of a decision if she felt the same way about him as he did about her.

Maybe she didn't, though. Maybe that was why she wanted to give the situation a lot of time and thought—which was exactly how she'd put it, too. ''A *lot* of time and thought,'' she'd said.

And if she really *wasn't* sure of her feelings, that would be part of the reason she didn't want them shouted to the world.

He considered that for a minute, then swore to

himself. After all these years of believing he'd never meet a woman he wanted to spend the rest of his life with, he'd done it. So what a kick in the head that she was nowhere near certain it was what she wanted.

When he focused on her again, she was checking one of the fax pages and punching a number into the phone.

"The insurance executive's got season tickets to the Blue Jays, remember?" she said, pressing the final number.

He nodded.

"Well, there was a home game last Wednesday night."

Before he could ask where she was intending to go with that, she held up her hand to stop him and said, "Mr. Bentley, please... Oh, he won't know my name, but tell him I'm on staff at the SkyDome."

There was a brief silence before she continued. "Mr. Bentley? I'm just calling to ask if you were using your seats last Wednesday? The Yankees game?

"You were?... Personally?... Oh, good, because someone found an umbrella under your seat, so we wanted to let you know that you can pick it up at... No? Oh, then whoever turned it in must have given us the wrong seat number. I'm sorry to have bothered you.

"Yes. You, too. 'Bye.

"Bingo," she added, clicking off. "Another one eliminated."

"Terrific," he said.

"You want to hear what else I thought up?"

"Of course."

"Well, it has to do with Harry Cochrane."

"He's the other top gun on our list, right?"

"Uh-huh. He's also the one who golfs eighteen holes just about every evening."

"So we establish whether he was golfing last Wednesday."

"Exactly."

When she shot him a smile that said he was an excellent student, he desperately wanted to kiss her again. But he didn't let himself move a muscle.

Fifteen minutes ago, he'd assumed he knew exactly where things stood between them. Now he wasn't at all sure. And he didn't like the way that made him feel.

"He golfs way up in Woodbridge," Anne was saying. "But I just don't see how we can do this one by phone. We'll have to drive up there and somehow get a look at the reservations book."

"Okay, let's go."

"Chase?" she said as he turned away.

When he turned back, she gazed at him for a moment. Then she murmured, "Something I said upset you. Whatever it was... Lord, we sure didn't pick the best circumstances for falling in love, did we?"

Exhaling slowly, he told himself he was the biggest idiot in the world. She loved him and he loved her. That was where things stood between them. And nothing else really mattered.

He stepped toward her, folded her into his arms, and simply held her. Maybe the circumstances weren't the best, but the way she made him feel was as good as it got.

CHAPTER THIRTEEN

THEY WERE HEADING UP Highway 27, expecting to reach Woodbridge in about ten minutes, when Chase's cell phone rang.

As he dug it out of his pocket, Anne said, "With any luck, that's my father. He promised to check in if he came up with something good."

Hoping Ben had something great, never mind good, Chase answered the phone.

"Your appraiser's been," the extortionist announced.

His hand tightened on the steering wheel. Just as they'd suspected he might, this guy had been watching the house.

Trying not to think about his being that near Julie and Rachel, he began slowing the Jeep and mouthed *extortionist* to Anne.

"Oh, Lord," she whispered.

"Yeah, well," the man continued. "Now that he's had his look, here's what we're gonna do. As soon as we're done talking, you call that manager of yours at the trust company and tell him you've gotta have the money today."

"But he can't—"

"Shut up! Just shut up and listen!" he snapped as Chase pulled off onto the shoulder.

"I've had it with waiting, so tell him to call the appraiser and check that you're getting approved for the mortgage. Once he's done that…well, tell him it's a matter of life and death. Or whatever. Just so it's today. Understand? Oh, and tell him twenties and fifties. Nothing else."

"Look," Chase said, his heart pounding in his ears. "*Possibly,* I could have it for you tomorrow. But there's no conceivable—"

"Either it's today or the cops get the gun. I'll call you later. If you have the money, we'll make the trade tonight. If not, your sister's lookin' at a long time behind bars."

The connection was abruptly broken.

"He's gone," Chase said, feeling positively sick. "And he says either he has the money tonight or that's it."

"You think he's bluffing?"

"Not a chance. But why would he suddenly decide it had to be right now?"

"Probably, the uncertainty just got too much for him. I mean, he's been walking a tightrope from the start. He wants that money. But if he *has* somehow tied the gun to Rachel, and figures it would give the cops 'proof' she's their killer… Well, we talked about this days ago."

Chase nodded, recalling the conversation virtually word for word. No matter how badly the guy wanted the money, part of him would be tempted to give that "proof" to the police so there'd be no risk of them ever looking for the *real* killer.

"At any rate," Anne was saying, "he must have reached the point of deciding that if he could be sure of the money, if he could get it tonight, that would be worth the risk of not clinching the case against Rachel. Otherwise, it wouldn't."

"He said he wanted only twenties and fifties," Chase told her. "Nothing else. Doesn't he realize what would happen if I actually asked a banker for that much money in small bills? It would take him about half a second to figure out what was going on and call the cops. So what if that dawns on this guy and—"

"No, if it hasn't by now, I doubt it will. He's got to be wound up so tightly that the only thing he can think about is getting his hands on the money.

"And remember what I said way back? That either he's smart enough to know you could *somehow* actually arrange to get two hundred thousand in cash, or he's doesn't know enough about how banks work to realize it would be difficult?"

"Uh-huh."

"Well, I guess now we know which he is—and that he's heard the 'unmarked twenties and fifties' line in too many movies. But, look, let me call my dad and update him."

Chase gave her the phone, wondering how many of their guesses about the guy were right and how many were wrong. If he wasn't the brightest bulb in the chandelier, would he actually have thought about linking trace evidence to the gun?

Maybe he would have. Or maybe his using the word *trace* had been nothing more than coincidence.

That was one of the major problems. They were dealing with far more unknowns than facts.

Anne finished leaving a message for her father, then punched in another number, saying, "Surely he'll have his cellular turned on."

Her whispered "Dammit" told him she'd gotten voice mail again.

She repeated her message, then passed the phone back, saying, "He must be meeting with someone and didn't want any interruptions. He'll check for messages as soon as he's done."

"And in the meantime?"

"I don't know. I have to think. But we've run out of time, so there's no point in going the rest of the way to Woodbridge."

"I'll turn around at the next exit," Chase said, pulling back onto the highway and gunning the engine. The extortionist's call had left him with a sense of urgency about getting home.

They made it about halfway back to the city before the phone rang once more.

"My father," Anne said.

He handed her the phone.

"Hello?" she answered. "Yes, just a sec," she added, passing it back to him. "It's Rachel."

"Hi," he said, his pulse racing. What if that damn

guy was still hanging around? If she'd spotted him, and—

"Chase, Mom just called again. To make sure I'd gotten through the funeral all right. And they want me and Julie to come up to Peterborough for a couple of days. She said she'd love you to come, as well, but…"

"Do you want to go?"

"I wouldn't mind. As crazy as her hovering sometimes makes me, I've decided I could use a little mothering. And you know how Dad's always got a hundred things he wants to do with Julie. That would be a lot better than her sitting around here, worrying about me."

"You're not too upset to drive?"

"No, I'd be okay."

"Then go. Just throw a few things in your car and hit the road." In case that guy *is* still hanging around. Or Dave Hustis shows up, wanting to talk.

"Are you sure you don't mind?"

"Of course not. Phone after you're there, okay? If I'm not home, just leave a message that you made it. And I'll call if I need to check anything. Or if there's something to report. Tell Julie I said to have a great time."

After their goodbyes, he clicked off and filled Anne in on what was happening—all the while praying "something to report" wouldn't prove to be that the police had gotten Graham's gun and were looking for Rachel.

BEN BARRETT HAD RETURNED Anne's call while she and Chase were still on the highway, and after she told him about the latest development they agreed to meet at her place.

Chase drove down his own street first, though, wanting to assure himself that Rachel and Julie were already on their way to Peterborough. Her car was gone, and he didn't see a stranger lurking anywhere. In fact, the street was virtually deserted, no neighbors in sight, let alone an extortionist.

That made him feel less anxious, although he was a long way from calm. Anticipating a showdown with a killer just didn't lend itself to feeling relaxed.

"I may as well leave the Jeep here," he said, pulling into his driveway.

Rather than just heading down the side of the house, they went through it. He was probably being paranoid, but he still felt spooked about that guy being right here spying.

Everything seemed fine inside, so after pausing to read a hastily scrawled "goodbye" note from Julie, they continued on to Anne's. When they got there, her father was standing out front, waiting for them.

He didn't bother with hellos, just said, "Has he called back yet?"

Chase shook his head.

"Well, while we're waiting we can discuss what you should say when he does. Although a lot will depend on what *he* says."

For the next hour they sat around the patio table

talking, and the best news Chase heard in the entire sixty minutes was that Ben owned a gun.

Canada's strict gun laws meant that even private investigators generally didn't carry one. And Ben was only licensed to carry his between his house and his gun club. He certainly intended to have it with him tonight, though. He'd said he'd go home and get it as soon as they'd heard from the extortionist.

The rest of the conversation wasn't as encouraging. They speculated on the various ways the guy might want to make the exchange, but until they heard exactly what he had in mind, the best they could do was settle on the bare bones of their own plan.

Basically, Chase would claim he had the money and arrange to trade it for the murder weapon. Then, as Ben put it, they'd "nail the guy and give him to the cops gift-wrapped—the ultimate citizen's arrest."

However, Chase had no delusions that "nailing" him would be anywhere near as easy as Ben made it sound. The guy would be armed.

Maybe few law-abiding Torontonians owned guns, but that wasn't true of the criminal element. And nobody in his situation was just going to roll over and play dead when he realized his plan was heading south.

Aside from that, they had something else to worry about. They still weren't sure whether this was a one-man show or they were actually dealing with two people—both of whom might turn up for the exchange.

Even three-to-one odds didn't make Chase happy; the thought that they might actually be three-to-two was twice as bad.

After they'd pretty well talked themselves out and were just waiting for the damned phone to ring, Chase sat surreptitiously looking at Anne and thinking she had to be far more nervous than she was letting on. Even though she'd told him that she knew self-defense, how much good would that do if things went seriously wrong?

He was working on convincing himself that fate wouldn't be cruel enough to let him find a woman like her, only to lose her, when his phone finally rang. The sound made him flinch.

"You'll do fine," Ben said. "Just listen to what he says and buy us enough time to work out a detailed plan."

He nodded. But buying a little more time was only step one. It was step two that could get them all killed.

His throat felt so dry he was surprised when his "Hello" actually came out.

"Did you get the money?"

He swallowed hard. "I'm picking it up just before closing time. That's at eight."

"Why not sooner?"

"The manager said they never have anything like two hundred thousand at his branch. That he'd have to arrange for a special delivery. We're lucky it's getting there tonight at all."

There was a pause, then the extortionist said, "You told him twenties and fifties?"

"Yes."

"You got something to write with?"

"Uh-huh." He grabbed the pen off the table and slid the pad closer.

"Okay, when you get the money put it in a sports bag."

"Right."

"And you know where the bus terminal is? Bay just above Dundas?"

"Yes."

"Okay, there's a bar called Harry's, south side of Dundas and west of Bay. Go into the stall in the men's room and take the top off the toilet. There'll be two keys taped to it."

"Uh-huh."

"Keys for lockers in the bus depot. And what you do first is lock the sports bag in the one with the lower number. I've got a duplicate key made, so just keep yours."

"Right."

"You've gotta buy a token from a machine to re-lock the locker, so be sure you have loonies."

As he checked his pocket for dollar coins, his caller continued.

"Once you lock up the sports bag, open the other locker. What you want is gonna be there—in a shoe box. Check that it's the genuine item, that the right initials are on it, then leave the terminal and walk back to your car. You got that?"

"Yes."

"Good, 'cuz I'm gonna be watching every move you make. And after you get to your car, drive straight home. Don't go anywhere else. Once you're home, the deal's done. You can do what you want with the item. Any questions?"

"No."

"Okay, then listen to what else I gotta say. If you phone the cops—"

"I won't! If I was going to do that I'd have done it the first time you called me."

"Fine. And don't get no ideas about bringing anyone along. You do this alone. Nobody but you is in your car. Nobody but you goes into that bar. Nobody but you goes into the bus terminal. And don't think you can pull a fast one, 'cuz I'll be watching. You try anything and—"

"I won't!"

"Do and you're dead."

ANNE'S FATHER HAD TOLD Chase to try to repeat everything the extortionist had said, and she could tell he was doing his best.

When he finished, Ben said, "You're sure it was '*I'm* gonna be watching every move' and '*I'll* be watching'? He never used the word *we?*"

"I'm sure."

"Good. That makes it far less likely we'll have two of them to contend with."

She nodded her agreement, although "far less likely" was no guarantee.

"But when you leave for downtown, be certain nobody's tailing you. If there *are* two, one might follow you. To see that you're not trying anything funny, that you really go get the money."

"Then should I pretend to?"

"What if he went from here?" Anne suggested. "If he took my car, he could just leave his Jeep parked in his driveway. I can take a taxi. That way, if someone's watching his street they'll be out of luck."

"Good thinking," her father said. "Do that, but still keep a sharp eye out," he added to Chase. "Although, even if there *are* two, they'll more likely stick together—both be waiting at the terminal."

"Because?"

"Because scumbags don't trust each other. If one suggested following you, the other would start thinking he might have a plan of his own. Like carjacking you a block from where you picked up the money.

"At any rate, if there are two, this could get complicated. But if there's only one, it should be pretty straightforward. And my gut's telling me there *is* only one."

Anne smiled at Chase, hoping she looked reassuring. And hoping even harder that her father's gut wasn't lying.

"My guess," he continued, "is the guy was in Harry's bar when he phoned you. And the minute you finished talking he went and taped the keys in the toilet.

"By now, he's probably at the terminal, watching

everyone who arrives and figuring that if you've got a double cross in mind he'll spot it being set up. Do you know the layout down there?''

Chase shook his head.

''Well, the lockers are in a long, tunnel-like corridor. You can enter it either from the waiting room or from the side street at the far end. One side is solid lockers and the other's the back wall of the bus bay. Its top half is glass, so people in the locker area can see both into the bay and across it into the waiting room.

''Now, we can't be sure which way he'll enter, but we'll probably have a good idea once you've picked up the keys. I assume the lockers number from the waiting-room end, and I'll bet the one you're supposed to put the bag in will have a really low number.

''That way, he'll be able to check that nothing's happening in the main part of the terminal before he opens the locker. But call me on my cellular before you leave that men's room. Then Anne and I will know exactly which locker needs watching.

''And here's how we'll play things. After you call, we'll position ourselves. Assuming I'm right about where the locker is, Anne will sit in the waiting room, looking as bored as the other passengers.''

''And you?'' she asked.

''I'll wear coveralls and give the impression I'm maintenance staff. That way, I'll be able to wander around without drawing much attention. And if anyone who actually works there asks what I'm doing,

I'll just say I'm a mechanic and came straight from work to meet a passenger."

He focused on Chase again, adding, "After you've been and gone, it'll simply be a matter of waiting to see who approaches the locker. And while he's getting the sports bag, I'll get him."

"After I leave, I should come back," Chase said. "I played a lot of football when I was a kid—developed a pretty mean tackle. And you might be glad of an extra body," he added, glancing at Anne.

His expression made her warm inside. It told her he wanted to be there in case she found herself in danger.

Her father, though, was already saying that once he was gone, he was gone.

"In the first place," he explained, "we can't be sure this guy won't follow you. It's not likely. Probably, he won't take his eyes off that locker, yet you never know.

"In the second place, we haven't entirely ruled out the possibility he has a partner."

"You said that if he did they'd stick together."

"I said that's *usually* how it goes. The problem is, we're having to guess about everything."

"They're educated guesses," Anne stressed, seeing how worried Chase seemed.

Her father nodded. "Still, we can't be one hundred percent sure about any of them. Which means, Chase, that when you leave, you drive home. Then, if someone *does* follow you, you've done what you were told."

"Ben, I—"

"Look, I know how much you want to be there. But we just can't risk it. Even if there's only one guy, and even if he doesn't follow you, he won't walk up to the locker right away. He'll keep an eye out for a while, convince himself things are completely safe before he makes his move. And if you come back and he spots you, he'll take off."

"But we'd have the gun by then. And we'd be able to tell the police the whole damn story."

"Yeah, only our lowlife would be on the loose—and so pissed off that he'd be out for revenge. You just don't take chances with a killer. Especially not when you've got a little girl at home."

"Ben, the more you talk about this... Dammit, as badly as I want this guy, the thought of you and Anne going up against him when he'll probably be armed to the teeth... When there could be two of them..."

"I can take care of myself. I've been doing it for a long time. And there's no way I'd let Anne get in the line of fire. We've worked together on stings before. We know what to expect from each other.

"We'll both be watching everything that's happening, trying to figure out who our boy is before he shows himself. And when he starts to make his move, while I'm concentrating on him, she'll be watching for anyone who seems interested in what he's doing. So if there *are* two of them, we'll know in time to modify the plan."

"But—"

"Chase, I'm not going to let my own daughter get hurt." He looked at her again.

"He never has before," she murmured.

CHASE STOOD WITH ANNE, watching Ben back out of her driveway. As he started down the street, she gave him a little wave, then closed the door. The moment she turned to him, Chase could see something was bothering her.

"What's the problem?" he said. "Afraid things will go wrong tonight?"

"Partly."

"And partly…?"

She shook her head. "It's so childish I hate to admit it."

"Go ahead. I've told you before, I'm used to childish."

"Well, it's…" She shrugged, then the rest of her words came tumbling out. "When he said he wasn't going to *let* me get hurt, it was the same as saying he'll have to be watching out for me. On top of everything else he'll have to worry about."

"Anne, you—"

"Chase, I *wanted* his help with this. I *need* it. But the way he completely took over and laid out the entire plan, as if I didn't… Oh, I told you it was childish. He's the expert—I'm not. It's just that…"

He drew her to him, breathing in the spring-meadow scent of her perfume and brushing a stray lock of silky hair back from her cheek.

"It's not childish," he told her. "He *did* take

charge. But isn't that the way he'd be with anyone? Calling the shots has to be second nature to him. And I really don't think he figured you needed the plan laid out for you. I didn't get that impression at all.''

She met his gaze. ''Really?''

''Really. It sounded to me as if he saw the two of you as a team. And when you said something, he listened. Like when you suggested I leave from here. Didn't he say that was a good idea?''

''Well…yes.''

''Anne, it was me he was laying things out for. I'm the rookie here.''

She continued to gaze at him for a few seconds, then whispered, ''Maybe you're right.''

''Hey, I'm almost always right,'' he teased. ''Haven't you realized that by now?''

Rather than answering, she simply rested her cheek against his chest and wrapped her arms around his waist. It started him wanting to make love with her so badly he could hardly believe it.

''We've got a while before we have to even think of calling a taxi for you,'' he murmured against her hair. ''Any particular way you'd like to kill the time?''

Easing back a little, she looked up at him again— and smiled a sexy smile.

''You haven't seen my office since I got it organized. Want to come upstairs and see?''

''Sure.''

He took her hand and led the way, but they didn't make it to her office. They didn't make it past her bedroom. And they were tearing each other's clothes off before they reached the bed.

"Oh, Chase," she whispered as he pulled her, naked, on top of him. "I want you so badly."

Not as badly as he wanted her. That wouldn't be possible.

He wrapped his arms around her, crushing her breasts to his bare chest, their soft fullness making him desperate to touch her all over.

Tangling her fingers in his hair, she kissed him hard on the mouth—a deep, soul-searching kiss— while her hair fell to either side of his face like a sweet-smelling curtain.

It shut out the rest of the world; only the two of them existed. He was aware of nothing but the length of her body pressed against his, moving with an unmistakable message of arousal, and the fierce pleasure of his erection hard against her belly.

Her kisses were intoxicating, her body hot and growing slick against his. He could feel her heart pounding and his own hammering in his chest.

"Now, Chase. I don't need any more time."

The words were half whisper, half moan, full of desire. He rolled onto his side, pulling her with him, and entered her with one firm thrust.

She inhaled sharply, then began to move in sync with him. Hot, tight, wet, wanting. Enough to make him crazy.

With each passing second, he grew nearer to the brink of insanity. Every time she whimpered against his throat, he came closer to climaxing.

When he finally did, it was shattering. He cried her name and the world exploded.

Suddenly, he was plunging through darkness at warp speed, spiraling downward, unable to breathe.

And then, just as he knew he was dying, he could feel his descent beginning to slow.

One ragged breath. Two. His body plastered to Anne's. Her breathing as shallow as his. Her hand on his arm, her head against his chest. The sweet release leaving him spent and the musky scent of sex enveloping them.

CHAPTER FOURTEEN

LYING WITH ANNE in the silence of her bedroom, the sheets tangled around them, all Chase could think was that, in a perfect world, they'd never have to move from where they were.

But in this world they did. They had to go to the damned bus terminal.

He shifted so that he could see her face, then traced her jaw softly with his fingers. It made her smile—and that made him smile.

He loved her so much. If anything awful happened to her tonight...

"Oh, Lord," she murmured.

"What?"

"You didn't use anything."

For a second he didn't know what she was talking about. Then it struck him and he said, "Oh, jeez, you're right. I'm sorry. You had me so crazy, I wasn't thinking. Is it...a risky time?"

"I'm not really sure. I've never used the rhythm method."

"Well..." He hesitated, fully aware of what she'd said about taking things slowly. Still, this might put the situation in a whole different light.

"Anne...don't say a word, okay? Just listen for a

minute. I love you. I want to marry you. Next week. Next month. Next year. Whenever we decide the timing's right. And if anything happens because of this... Well, I think having a baby would be great. I mean, if you'd like one, too.''

For a moment she merely gazed at him. Then she smiled again and he could feel his entire being light up.

"I'd adore one," she said. "I'd just prefer it to be a planned event."

He cuddled her closer and kissed the pulse at the base of her throat. Then he began working his way downward, her skin baby smooth against his lips.

"That *was* a marriage proposal, wasn't it?" she whispered.

He raised his head and smiled. "Definitely."

"Good. I just wanted to be sure I heard right."

He was about to go back to kissing her when the doorbell rang.

They both tensed.

"If you don't answer, they'll leave," he said.

"What if it's my dad come back? I'd better go see."

She grabbed her robe from the chair and tugged it on as she headed along the hall—praying it wasn't her father. He'd take one look at her and know exactly what had been going on. And that wasn't the way she wanted him to learn that she and Chase were in love.

But when she opened the door she almost wished

it *was* him. Because two men were standing there and one was holding up a police ID.

"I'm Detective Westin, Toronto police," he said. "This is my partner, Detective Providence. We're looking for Chase Nicholson. Is he here?"

For an instant she considered what might happen if she told the truth. If they wanted to talk to him at length it would keep him from getting to the bus terminal.

"No," she said. "He's not."

"Oh?" Westin said. "His next-door neighbor told us she saw him over here in the yard not long ago—talking with you and an older man."

"Ah, yes, he was here, but he's gone. They're both gone."

"I see. Do you have any idea when he'll be home?"

She shook her head.

"You wouldn't happen to know where Rachel Nicholson is, would you?"

She thought for another split second, then lied again—telling herself it wasn't *exactly* a lie, because she didn't know specifically where in Peterborough Rachel was.

"Well, if you hear from her, please ask her to give me a call." Westin handed her a card.

"Yes, I'll do that. But…Rachel and I are friends. I know you've talked to her before, and… This isn't serious, is it?"

Westin shook his head. "We just want to ask her a few more questions."

"Fine. When I see her I'll tell her to phone you."

She watched the detectives start down the walk, then closed the door, a chill creeping through her.

Their wanting to ask Rachel more questions was *not* a good sign. In fact, it might well mean they'd built a strong-enough case against her to lay charges. And that was without even having the damned murder weapon.

"Who was it?" Chase asked, buttoning his shirt as he headed down the stairs.

She simply stared at him, a whole series of terrifying questions snaking around in her mind.

Had those two been looking for Rachel because she was guilty after all? And if so, what would that do to Chase and Julie? To Chase and her?

WHEN JULIE ARRIVED back with Grandpa, Grandma and Rachel were sitting at the kitchen table. There was a piecrust made, and they were peeling apples.

"She beat me," Grandpa announced. "I golf three times a week, but my granddaughter comes up here and an hour later she's beating the pants off me at miniature golf."

Julie smiled. "I didn't beat the pants off you. I only won by two strokes."

"Well, I'm just glad none of my golfing buddies were there to see it. They'd never have let me live it down."

"I take it you had a good time?" Grandma said to Julie.

"Uh-huh. We went for ice cream after. Double scoops."

"Roger," Grandma said, giving Grandpa a look. "You know it's almost dinnertime."

"That's okay," Rachel said. "It only means that Julie won't have any room for dessert. But you don't like Grandma's apple pie, anyway, do you," she teased.

It made Julie smile again. They hadn't been here long, but Rachel already seemed a whole lot happier.

"Do I have time for a nap before dinner?" Grandpa asked.

At Grandma's nod, he said, "Then I'll see you three in half an hour."

As he headed off, Julie wandered over to the table and sat down. She snuck a slice of apple and ate it, trying to decide exactly what to say.

Sometimes, if Penelope Snow wanted to find out something from adults, she just got them talking. It was harder to do in real life than in Anne's books, though.

In real life, you had to ask the right questions or they got going on the wrong stuff. But she didn't think she'd better come right out and ask if Rachel thought Daddy was gonna marry Anne.

Finally, she said, "Grandma, did Rachel tell you who our new neighbor is?"

When Grandma shook her head, Rachel said, "Behind us, in the Kitchners' house."

Julie was kind of surprised she hadn't already told Grandma about Anne, but maybe that was 'cuz she didn't want Grandma to know Anne was helping her—didn't want Grandma to know she still *needed* help.

After the first day or so, the TV people had just started saying there'd been no arrest in the case. They hadn't been talking about Graham's girlfriend anymore. So maybe Grandma thought everything was okay now.

"And who is the new neighbor?" she was asking.

"Her name's Anne Barrett and she writes kids books. Mysteries. Ones I like."

"Oh, that's interesting. Is she nice?"

Julie nodded, then glanced at Rachel. "Right?"

"Yes, she's very nice."

"Well, that's good."

Julie waited for one of them to say something more. They didn't, so she said, "Daddy thinks she's nice, too."

"Oh?" Grandma glanced at Rachel.

Rachel looked at Julie.

"Well, he *does*."

"Yes, of course he does, hon."

When they went quiet again, Julie frowned. She could ask how *much* Rachel thought he liked Anne, but there had to be something better.

"That's why he couldn't come with us," she said at last. "'Cuz he's doing stuff with Anne."

"Oh?" Grandma glanced at Rachel a second time.

"It's an involved story," Rachel said, shooting Julie one of her "drop it" looks.

"How long ago did she move in?" Grandma asked.

"Not very," Rachel told her.

Julie waited again, but they just weren't cooperating. Finally, she gave up and said, "I think Daddy *really* likes her. Don't you, Rachel? I think he might even ask her to marry him."

The house was suddenly as quiet as in the middle of the night.

"What makes you think that, hon?" Rachel asked at last.

She shrugged. "I just do."

"Then it's a good thing she's nice," Grandma said slowly.

"Uh-huh. But it would be kind of funny, wouldn't it. I mean, Rachel does the cooking and all that stuff. So there wouldn't be anything for Anne to do if she lived with us."

"Hon…" Rachel said. "I don't think your dad actually has any ideas about getting married. But he might, sometime in the future. And if that happens, I'd probably go live somewhere else."

Her eyes began to sting and her throat suddenly hurt. She'd known that was what would happen!

"Julie," Rachel said softly. "Take it easy. We're only talking 'ifs' and 'maybes' here. And…you know how much I love you."

She nodded, trying not to cry.

"Well, then you know I'll always be part of your life. And you'll always be part of mine. But nothing stays exactly the same forever. That's just the way things are. So, whether your dad ever gets married again or not, someday I'll probably be living somewhere else.

"I mean, what if *I* got married? Then I'd be living with my husband. I wouldn't stop loving you, though."

"But I need you!"

"Oh, darling." Grandma scooted her chair closer so she could give Julie a hard hug. "Julie, whatever happens, your father will make sure everything's all right for you. You know that, don't you?"

She sniffed, and said she guessed she did. But what if there was something he couldn't make right?

"And you know what else?"

"What?"

"In no time, you'll be old enough that you won't need Rachel or anyone else doing things for you very often. When she and your dad were growing up, it seemed as if one day I was spending every minute looking after them and the next day they hardly needed me at all. They could do almost everything for themselves.

"But that didn't mean we stopped loving one another. It's just…as Rachel said, things change. Nothing stays the same forever."

"But I want this to!"

"Oh, Julie." Grandma brushed her hair back from her face. "Darling, if everything always stayed the same life would be awfully boring. And if your dad ever does get married again, whether to this Anne or someone else, it'll just be different for a while, that's all.''

"It might be awful!"

"Hon, nobody would want it to be awful," Rachel said. "Not your dad, and not you, and not whomever he married. So if you were all trying to make it good, then it wouldn't be awful at all."

"Well…I guess *maybe* it wouldn't."

"Have I ever lied to you before?" Rachel teased.

She tried to smile, but couldn't. Then she started thinking about the stuff Anne had told her this morning.

"Know what?" she said at last.

"What?" Rachel asked.

"Anne's mom died when she was real little. And her dad never got married again. And now she wishes he had, 'cuz she thinks he's lonely."

"Then maybe that's something to keep in mind, darling," Grandma said. "Because no matter how much you love your dad, you'll eventually grow up and move away."

"I might not."

"You will, Julie. Just like he and Rachel moved away from Grandpa and me. And if I didn't have your grandfather, I know I'd be lonely. So if your father does fall in love with someone, and she's nice…"

Julie considered that. Anne *was* nice. And she wasn't just pretending, either. Not like Susie Malinsky's stepmother, who only acted nice until after she married Susie's father.

If Anne married her dad, she'd keep on being the way she was now. Deep down, Julie just knew she would. And even though it would be sad not to have Rachel living there, what she said was true. It wouldn't mean they'd stop loving each other. So maybe it wouldn't be *too* sad.

"Hon?" Rachel said.

"Uh-huh?"

"After we get home, let's talk to your dad about this, all right?"

She nodded, remembering how, the other morning, he'd asked her if she liked Anne. And she'd said that Anne was only "okay."

Maybe, when they got home, she'd better tell him she hadn't really meant that.

BEFORE ANNE LEFT for the bus terminal, she'd made sandwiches. Neither she nor Chase had managed to eat more than a couple of bites, though, and after her taxi disappeared down the street he wandered back into the kitchen and stood staring at the remains on the table. Then his gaze shifted to the phone.

He wanted to call his parents' place and talk to everyone, but knew he couldn't.

Not that he'd say anything about those detectives looking for Rachel. That could wait until tonight was over. Then, hopefully, they'd have their *real* killer.

But regardless of what he said, his family would probably pick up on how anxious he was. And that would only make them worry.

Absently, he began sticking things in the dishwasher, recalling what Ben had told him. Once he left the terminal, his role in their sting was over. If he came back and the extortionist spotted him, it would blow everything.

Rationally, he realized that made sense. Even so, the prospect of simply walking out and driving home, of not knowing what was happening to Anne until things were over and done with…

He just wasn't sure how he could force himself to do that. On the other hand, if he screwed up and their guy took off, hot for revenge…

He dug his wallet from his pocket and flipped to a picture of Julie. Merely looking at it and imagining a killer out to get her sent his anxiety level through the ceiling.

This plan simply *had* to work. There was too much at stake for anything to go wrong.

Yet what if something did? What if their guy *did* have a partner? Two scumbags with guns might be more trouble than Ben and Anne could handle.

After considering the situation for another couple of minutes, he headed over to his own house and grabbed a few things. When he got back to Anne's it was still early, but since he was feeling too antsy to wait any longer, he scooped her keys off the counter, picked up the sports bag they'd filled with cut-up newspapers and strode out to her car.

With Ben's warning in mind, he kept checking the rearview mirror as he drove—until he was satisfied that no one was tailing him. Less than half an hour after he left Anne's he was cruising the streets near the bus terminal, watching for an empty parking space.

He spotted one on Elm, only a short block away, and sat in the car until eight-thirty. Then, his throat so dry it was itchy, he climbed out and walked down to Dundas, sweating heavily enough that the straps of the sports bag were slippery by the time he reached Harry's bar.

It was the sort of hole-in-the-wall you found near bus terminals in all big cities, its air thick with the smell of beer and cigarette smoke. And although it wasn't a place *he'd* have picked to leave anything, when he made his way to the men's room the keys were where they were supposed to be.

They were numbers four and seventy-six, which meant Ben had been right. The locker he was to leave the money in had to be right at the waiting-room end of the tunnel.

He called Ben's cellular number and reported in. Then he replaced the top of the toilet and headed out onto the street again—where the muggy downtown air now seemed positively fresh.

After waiting for a streetcar to rumble past, he dodged the rest of the traffic on his way back across Dundas, his adrenaline pumping like crazy. By the time he walked into the terminal, his heart was racing.

The ticket windows were on the left-hand side of the entrance lobby. To his right was a waiting area with rows of green vinyl chairs.

A sign pointed him in the direction of the lockers,

and as he started across the tile floor he let his gaze drift over the people in the chairs. Anne wasn't among them.

However, when he reached the next section of the waiting room he spotted her—sitting where she had a bird's-eye view of the entrance to the lockers. In her jeans and sneakers, with her hair pulled back into a ponytail, she looked about fourteen.

Aware that the extortionist might already be watching him, he eyed her for only a moment before heading over to a token machine and purchasing a token. That done, he walked into the long corridor of lockers.

His fingers trembling a little, he dug the key to number four out of his pocket, opened the locker and stashed the bag inside. Then he closed the door, stuck the token in the slot to relock it and put the key back in his pocket.

Feeling eyes boring into him, he started along toward number seventy-six. That was the one with the gun inside.

His fingers trembling even worse this time, he opened it. When he pulled out the plastic bag with a shoe box inside, it was heavier than he'd been expecting.

The extortionist's instructions echoing in his head, he checked the box's contents. Sure enough, it contained a pistol. The initials on the handle were G.V.L.—for Graham Vincent Lowe.

BY LOOKING THROUGH the windows of the waiting room and across to those along the corridor of lockers, Anne was able to watch Chase until he finished in there and headed out onto the street at the far end.

Once he disappeared, she focused on the doorway leading to the lockers—and prayed that no one would go after him. Because on her way here she'd thought of a possibility that was absolutely terrifying.

She didn't know why it hadn't occurred to her earlier. Especially when, more than once, she and Chase had talked about how the real killer had to be tempted to give the police his "proof" of Rachel's guilt.

What if he'd devised a plan that would let him do just that? Let him end up with both the money for himself and Graham's gun for the cops?

How would things play out if he went after Chase, intent on retrieving the gun? Or if his accomplice followed Chase, if there actually were two of them?

Chase would end up dead before he ever got back to the car; that's how things would undoubtedly play out.

She licked her dry lips as a man strode rapidly into the locker area—a scruffy young man in worn jeans and cowboy boots. Who might or might not be a killer. Who might or might not be following the man she loved.

He wasn't carrying anything, which bothered her. Most people in the waiting room had at least a back-pack. But as desperately as she wanted to go after him, she couldn't.

She had to stay where she was. Deviating from the

plan would mean leaving her father on his own. Besides, most likely the corridor simply afforded a shorter route to wherever Mr. Cowboy Boots was going. Which meant she should stop worrying and think about something else entirely.

She didn't like where her thoughts went next, though. They flashed back to how shocked she'd been when she'd opened her front door and found Westin and Providence standing there. And to how they might well have come looking for Rachel because they were intending to charge her.

Then the still-unanswered question raised its ugly head once more. Was Rachel actually guilty? Even though Anne didn't want to believe that was even within the realm of the conceivable?

She ordered herself to forget about Rachel for the time being. And not to think about Chase, either. She had to concentrate on the job. Otherwise, she might miss something.

After spending a few seconds adjusting her mental set, she glanced toward the windows that faced the bus bay. Her father, in dark coveralls, was standing beside a half-full bus and talking to its driver. But he was positioned so he could see both into the waiting room and through the windows along the corridor of lockers.

Knowing he wouldn't miss a thing, she casually let her gaze roam the room, hoping to see someone focused on the locker that Chase had put the sports bag into. When she didn't, she glanced at her father once more.

He didn't meet her gaze, but he raised his hand to cover a fake yawn—a signal that he figured they might be in for a long wait.

ANNE'S FATHER HAD GUESSED right. Dusk was closing in around the bus terminal before their guy finally made his move.

He was somewhere in his late twenties, with a solid build and shaggy brown hair. Anne decided he had to be their man before he was halfway across the waiting room.

Her first clue was that, just like Mr. Cowboy Boots, he wasn't carrying anything. Her second was that he had on a denim jacket, even though the terminal was stuffy and it still had to be hot and humid outside. Assuming she was reading things right, his jacket would be concealing a gun.

Rubbing her damp palms against her jeans, she gazed out into the bus-bay area for long enough to assure herself that her father had spotted him, too. Then she began slowly scanning the rest of the people within her range of vision. If he wasn't alone, his partner would be watching every step he took. But nobody seemed to be paying him any attention.

Okay, that was good. If he was alone they should be just fine.

When she glanced at her father again, he was heading into the waiting area. Her heart began beating faster as she watched him walk halfway to the tunnel, then stop and begin searching his pockets.

He'd wait right there, she knew—far enough from

their guy not to worry him but close enough to make his move.

The extortionist would open the locker and remove the bag. A moment after he started walking away, her father's gun would be in his back and that would be the end of things. Unless something went wrong.

It won't, she told herself firmly.

Their guy reached the locker, then looked carefully in either direction. Rapidly, she scrutinized the waiting room a final time.

Once she'd assured herself he really was on his own, she turned back toward the windows and watched, not breathing, as he opened the locker door.

Then her peripheral vision caught a movement, and when she glanced to her left Dave Hustis was walking toward the tunnel.

In a split-second freeze-frame her brain added things together. Dave *was* the dirty cop! This guy's partner in crime! But her father wouldn't know who Dave was, so she had to warn him there were two of them.

"Dave!" she called, standing up. "It's Dave Hustis, isn't it?"

He stopped dead. Not ten feet away, his partner pulled the bag from the locker.

An instant later, someone flew out of nowhere and brought Dave down with a flying tackle.

CHAPTER FIFTEEN

THEIR GUY TOOK OFF running down the corridor of lockers, the sports bag clutched to his chest and Anne's father in pursuit.

Dave Hustis was on the floor, pinned beneath whoever had tackled him but struggling to get free.

Anne hurried toward the two men as quickly as she could, pushing past people gathering to watch the excitement. Dave would have a gun, but if he got it out she might be able to grab it before anyone could get hurt.

"Chase!" he yelled as she neared them. "Chase! It's me! Dave Hustis!"

She jolted to a stop beside them, realizing it really was Chase. In different clothes than earlier. And a baseball cap lying on the floor. A rudimentary disguise.

"Dammit, let me up," Dave hollered. "He'll get away."

"But you won't," Chase snapped.

Dave uttered an obscenity, then said, "Listen to me! I'm on your side!"

The next instant, a beefy security guard was looming over them, bellowing, "Okay, that's enough. Take it outside."

He grabbed Chase by the upper arms and yanked him backward. As he stumbled, then tried to gain his balance when the guard let go, Dave scrambled to his feet and sped off into the corridor.

"Chase," Anne cried, "they'll kill my father."

Without another word, they headed full tilt after Dave. When they reached the far end and roared out into the gathering twilight, he was just turning onto Dundas. They raced the few hundred yards to the corner and wheeled around it.

"There's my dad," Anne cried, catching a glimpse of him charging along a block in front of them.

Ignoring a red light and the screeching of brakes, they dashed across the first intersection they hit and on toward the next—dodging the occasional pedestrian in their path.

Her heart was pounding, but she kept running as fast as she could, unable to think about anything except the fact that her father was chasing one man with a gun and another one was on his tail.

Up ahead, Dave reached University Avenue and cut to his right, vanishing behind the building on the corner. By the time they got there, not one of the three men was visible.

Utter panic seized her. Then Chase pointed at the lit transit sign and said, "The subway! They've gone down into the subway."

Of course! The glossy green tiles of the entrance walls were mere feet from where they stood.

Chase grabbed her hand and they headed down the

stairs so quickly that she stumbled and almost fell before they made it to the bottom.

"This way," he said, half dragging her along the passageway leading into the station.

There was still no sign of the others.

"Chase, maybe they didn't come down here!"

"They must have." He swung himself over a turnstile, then reached back to help her.

As they raced for the staircase that would take them to the subway platform, the lone ticket taker was screaming at them to come back and pay.

They started downward again, a rush of stale air blowing up at them and Anne feeling certain she'd never been more frightened. What if Dave and his partner had subdued her father—or worse—and were now lying in wait for them on the platform?

They'd just reached the first of two landings when half a dozen people began scurrying up the stairs.

"Don't go down there," one said in passing. "There's weird stuff going on."

Oh, Lord. Whatever the weird stuff was, her father had to be in the thick of it. Yet when they reached the platform it was completely deserted.

She stared at the gaping black hole the tracks disappeared into, thinking her father would never in a million years have gone into a subway tunnel. But if he hadn't, where was he?

Then, just as Chase said "Where did they go?" her father whispered, "Anne?"

She jumped—half frightened to death, half flooded with relief that he was all right—and before she had time to turn around he'd grabbed her arm from behind and was pulling her into the space beneath the stairs.

"Get back here where you can't be seen," he said. "Our guy dove off the platform and he's holed up in the tunnel."

While he was adding "You get in here, too," to Chase, she spotted Dave standing by the far wall of the space, talking on a cell phone.

"But..." Chase gestured toward Dave, wondering what the hell was going on.

Ben shrugged. "We haven't really had time to chat. All we've established is that I'm a P.I. and he wasn't chasing that sleazoid because they're buddies."

"Okay," Dave said, putting the phone in his pocket. "They're stopping the trains and I've called for backup. All that's left to do is make sure he stays in the tunnel until it arrives."

"He won't dare stick his head out into the light," Ben said. "He'd be momentarily blinded, but we wouldn't."

Dave nodded. "Yeah, I think you're right. We'll have to fish him out. It won't be tough, though. One team'll go in from here and one from the next station. He'll be the tuna in the sandwich.

"But you're working for *them?*" he added, his glance taking in Anne and Chase.

"Not exactly working for them," Ben explained. "Just helping out. She's my daughter."

"Wait a minute," Chase said. "You aren't involved with that guy? You really *are* on our side?"

"I don't know why you figured I wasn't, but never mind that now. I need you to tell me who he is. And exactly what was going on in the bus terminal."

"How did you end up there?" Chase said.

For a moment Dave looked as if he was going to say that *he* got to ask the questions. But then he said, "I stopped by your place, hoping Rachel had decided to talk to me about the night Graham was killed. And when no one answered the door, I remembered that Anne lived right behind you.

"So, on the off chance you and Rachel were at her place, I drove around to the next street—just in time to see you coming out of the house with that bag and driving off in what I assumed was Anne's car. And my instincts told me something strange was going on, so I tailed you."

"But I kept checking that I wasn't being followed."

"Well, when I follow people they're not supposed to notice. At any rate, I tagged along while you went into that bar, then to the bus terminal. And when I spotted Anne waiting there, I *knew* something was up."

"I didn't see you," she said. "And I was watching the crowd."

He shrugged to say that no one was supposed to notice him in a crowd, either, then continued his explanation. "I figured the two of you might be in over your heads, so I hung around. And when that guy went for the bag, I thought I'd keep you out of trouble by intercepting him before you could. I wasn't counting on you trying to maim me for my effort," he added to Chase.

"Sorry about that."

"You weren't even supposed to be there," Ben reminded him. "You should have been long gone."

"Yeah...well..." He looked at Anne, and the way she smiled made him awfully glad he'd been there for her. Even if, as was obviously the case, he'd jumped to some wrong conclusions.

"What did you take from the other locker?" Dave said.

The question caught him off guard. In the excitement, he'd forgotten about the gun. Now, though...

One glance at Anne's father told him that even if he wanted to lie there'd be no point. Either he'd tell Dave the truth or Ben would.

But what if the extortionist really *had* doctored the gun? Turned it into "evidence" that Rachel had killed Graham?

If he eluded the police and escaped from that tunnel, the truth might never surface.

IT WAS THREE in the morning before the police detectives interviewing Anne said that she could go home. By then, she'd told them every single detail of her involvement in what had happened—beginning with the morning Julie had wandered into her backyard and ending on the subway platform.

When one of the two men escorted her downstairs,

to the front lobby of police headquarters, Chase, her father and Dave Hustis were all there waiting. Obviously, their interviews had gone more quickly than hers.

Her father spotted her first, and a second later he was wrapping his arm around her shoulders, saying, "You look exhausted."

"That's only because I am."

"Well, the good news is they got that guy out of the subway and nobody was hurt. They're questioning him now."

"Do they think he's our killer?" she asked Dave.

"I don't know yet. Given what your father and Chase have been telling me, though, it sounds to *me* as if he is.

"But, look, why don't I give the three of you a lift to where you left your cars? I'll just shoot down to the garage and pick you up out front in a couple of minutes."

He took a step away, then turned back toward the other men and added, "I'm glad you had time to fill me in. That was quite the story."

As he started off again, her father said, "Do you still get nightmares when you're overtired?"

"Sometimes," she admitted.

"Then why don't I drive you home and spend what's left of the night in your spare bedroom. That be okay?"

She couldn't stop herself from glancing at Chase. She wanted to spend what was left of the night in his arms. But she knew precisely how her father was feeling, because she felt the same way.

He'd been so worried about something awful happening to her that he couldn't quite believe it hadn't. Just as she'd been so worried about him and Chase.

"You'll drive Anne's car back?" he said to Chase.

"Sure."

The bus terminal was mere blocks from police headquarters, so they were all on their way home in no time. Her father drove in silence for a bit, then said, "We didn't do too badly, eh? Considering we haven't worked together in a long time."

"Well...*you* didn't do too badly. I didn't spot Dave until the last second. And Chase was right in front of me before I realized he'd come back."

"Everybody misses things, darling."

"I know, but..."

"But?"

She shrugged wearily, aware she wouldn't have gone an inch down this road if her brain wasn't dead tired.

"Anne? What's the matter?"

"Nothing."

"Nothing? Come on, darling, I know you better than that."

She didn't want to say anything more, but she knew him as well as he knew her. And he wasn't going to let this drop until he got an explanation.

"I guess..." she said at last. "Well, it doesn't really matter at this point, but I guess I've just always wished I'd been a better investigator than I was."

"What do you mean, *better?* What more do you think you could have done on this case than you did?"

"Dad, I really don't want to talk about it, okay?"

"Then just listen for a minute. You figured out the motives someone might have had for killing Graham. Then you got the information on the counterfeiters and... We simply ran out of time, that was all. And even so we got the guy."

"Yes. *We* did. You and Dave and Chase and me. I could never have done it alone and... Oh, what I'm really trying to say is that I know you always wished I..." She shook her head, regretting having started this more with each word she spoke.

"I wished what?"

"What I mean...I know that when we were working together I was never as good as you hoped I'd be. That's all I mean."

"Anne," he said quietly, "you were fine."

"Sure," she murmured. "You were never once disappointed in me."

"That's true. Never once. Honey, when you were working with me I wouldn't have traded you for anyone. Not even Sherlock Holmes."

She swallowed hard and met his gaze. "Honestly?"

"Honestly. Maybe you weren't the best investigator in the whole wide world, but you were pretty damned good—and you always tried your hardest.

"Besides, look at you now. A successful author, for Pete's sake. And that guy you helped catch tonight is probably a murderer. How many authors do you think could manage that?''

"Well..." Her throat was too tight to go on. She could tell he'd meant every word he'd said. So, for all these years, she'd been thinking far worse of herself than he thought of her.

"Darling," he said, reaching over and covering her hand with his, "I've never been anything but proud of you."

CHASE CALLED RACHEL at dawn to tell her their extortionist was in custody—and that Dave figured he was the killer. Two hours later, she and Julie arrived home.

At the moment, Julie was next door playing with Becky while he and Rachel were sitting beside the phone with the TV on—hoping, one way or the other, to hear the latest developments.

"Chase?" she said when the news channel went to commercial.

"Uh-huh?"

"Julie told Mom and me that she figures you're going to marry Anne."

"Oh?" He tried to sound as if the idea had never occurred to him, but knew he'd failed when Rachel said, "You're in love with her, aren't you."

"Well...yeah. I was going to leave talking about it until after things quieted down, though. And—"

"Hey, don't look so worried. I think she's terrific. And Julie does, too."

"I'm not so sure about that. A few things she's said have got me concerned."

"I don't think you need to be. She's just afraid of change, like ninety-nine percent of the people in the world."

"Including you? If I did get married, life would be different for all of us."

She gave him a slow shrug. "Chase, living here has been great. And you know how much I love you and Julie. But facing the possibility of spending the next however many years in jail...well, that really got me thinking how little I've been doing with my life.

"I should be trying harder to get my career going. And developing more outside interests. Otherwise, I'm going to wake up one day and find..."

She shrugged again. "The bottom line is that the last thing you should worry about is what I'll do. Because I've started to think I'm ready to move on, anyway."

"Rachel..." He paused, the lump in his throat taking him by surprise.

"But getting back to Julie," she said. "Mom and I talked to her for a while and I'm sure she'll be fine. All she'll need is some reassurance from you and Anne."

"You're *really* sure?"

"Uh-huh. That's what my intuition's telling me, and you know how reliable it is."

He smiled, a sense of relief seeping through him.

Then she gestured toward the television and said, "Look, here's something now."

An interior shot of the St. Patrick station had appeared on the screen and the announcer was saying, "CFTV has just received an update on last night's subway arrest. According to an unnamed source, the man who attempted to elude police by hiding in the University Avenue subway tunnel is a suspect in the recent High Park murder of Toronto police detective Graham Lowe."

"Oh, thank heavens," Rachel murmured. "Hearing it on the news makes it seem much more real."

He nodded, but they weren't entirely out of the woods yet. They needed more than an "unnamed source" and a "suspect" for that.

"Chase, do you think this means—" She stopped speaking as the phone began to ring. A few moments after she answered, she said, "I know. We were watching, too. And, yes, I *am* happy. I only wish there'd been more details.

"Uh-huh, he's right here. It's Anne," she told Chase.

"Hi," he said, taking the phone.

"Hi. Good news, huh?"

"Absolutely. Why don't you come over and we'll celebrate."

"My dad's still here."

"Bring him with you. You know Rachel wants to thank him."

"Well…"

Turning away from Rachel, he whispered, "And I've got some other good news."

"Me, too," Anne said. "So, okay, we'll be right there."

Mere minutes later, they'd introduced Ben to Rachel and he was giving her *his* version of last night's excitement.

Chase caught Anne's eye, then casually wandered out of the family room. After saying something to the others, she followed him.

When she walked into the kitchen, he wrapped his arms around her and kissed her.

"Do you really have good news, or was that just a ruse to get me over here?" she teased when he let her go.

"No, I really do. Julie told Rachel and my mother that she thinks we're going to get married. And they figure she'll be fine with it."

Anne smiled. "That *is* good. How about Rachel?"

"Same thing."

He kissed her again, then said, "And your news?"

"Well…I was worried about whether we had the rhythm method on our side or not, so I called a friend who's a nurse. And she said there's almost no chance I'm pregnant. Which means we won't have any reason to rush things. We can take our time and—"

"But what if I want to rush?" he whispered against her lips. "What if I want to marry you so badly I can't think straight? What if—"

"Chase?" Rachel called. "Anne? Dave Hustis is here."

ANNE MENTALLY GAVE DAVE points for being cool. He had to be surprised that both she and her father were at the Nicholsons', but he didn't show it in the least.

"I've just come from talking to Westin and Providence," he announced once they were all sitting in the family room. "And I figured you'd appreciate hearing where things stand."

Rachel shot him a smile. "You figured right."

"Well, okay, most of this will be released to the media shortly, but for the moment it's confidential."

Everyone nodded.

"The guy we nailed last night definitely killed Graham."

"You're sure?" Ben asked.

"Uh-huh. They've got a signed confession."

"Thank heavens," Rachel whispered.

"Graham's wallet and his most recent computer disk were in the perp's apartment," Dave continued. "Along with an electronic voice-altering device— which would have been what he used when he called you, Chase.

"But the clincher was that the Emergency Task Force fellows recovered the murder weapon from the subway tunnel. Our boy had it with him last night and tried to lose it.

"With all that for ammunition, getting a confession wasn't real tough. Oh, and the disk had a lot of fresh information on it. Enough that the counterfeit task force should be able to nail the major players."

"So the gun our guy left in that locker wasn't the real item," Chase said.

"Well, it was and it wasn't. It was Graham's, all right. But ballistics did its thing on both guns, and the perp's was the murder weapon."

"Then my idea about the trace evidence was all wet," Anne said. "There'd have been no point in trying to make it look as if Rachel had handled Graham's gun. It wouldn't have mattered whether she had or not."

"But given the way he used the word *trace* it was a good hypothesis," her father said.

When she looked at him he added, "And *none* of us guess right all the time. Not even Sherlock Holmes."

She couldn't help smiling, then she turned her attention back to Dave.

"At any rate," he was saying, "the guy simply stepped out of the trees and shot Graham—which explains why there was no sign of a struggle. Then he took Graham's gun, along with the rest of the items, from his body."

"And was the killing related to the counterfeiting case?" Ben asked.

"Uh-huh. You folks had that right. Our boy—his name is Wayne Kuzak, by the way—was a low-level member of the ring. A runner."

"Which was what Graham posed as," Anne said.

"Right."

"Wayne Kuzak is one of the names we had," Ben said. "One I hadn't begun checking out yet."

"Well, he suspected that Graham was a cop," Dave continued. "And tailed him for a while to find out for sure.

"That's how he knew who his girlfriend was," he added, glancing at Rachel. "He'd followed Graham here when he was picking you up. Then, I guess, after the extortion idea struck him, it wasn't hard to learn a little more about your situation.

"You also had that one right," he added to Anne. "Trying for the money was just an afterthought. But getting back to the murder, once he established Graham actually was a cop, he decided to take him out. Otherwise, since Graham could ID him, he'd have ended up in jail. Plus, he knew that getting rid of an infiltrator would make the controlling members of the ring sit up and take notice.

"So, as you figured, he was following Graham the evening of the murder, hoping for a good opportunity to kill him, and he got one."

When Dave fell silent, Chase said, "Okay if I ask you something?"

"Sure."

"Why were you trying so hard to make Rachel talk to you about what happened in the park?"

"Because I wanted to do anything I could to help put that lowlife away. And I suspected she'd actually witnessed the murder—was just too frightened to admit it when she talked to Westin and Providence. I thought the killer might have told her she'd be next if she opened her mouth. But if she'd felt she could trust me, as a friend…

"Trusting you had nothing to do with it," she told him. "I honestly didn't see anyone. If I had, I'd have said so in the beginning."

"What about the story Kuzak used to intimidate them?" Anne asked. "Saying that he'd know if Chase contacted the police?"

"That he'd know right away," Chase put in. "As I told you last night, he made it sound as if he had a pipeline—which is partly what had us convinced there might be a crooked cop involved."

"Well, I asked about that, but as far as they know Kuzak was working alone."

"If he'd had a partner," Ben said, "he'd have been shouting that to the world when he confessed his own sins."

Dave nodded. "Which means he wouldn't actually have had a clue if Chase had reported him."

"But if there was no dirty cop, why was Graham keeping his notes on disk?" Rachel asked. "Who was he afraid would try to see them?"

"That could be one of those things we'll never know," Dave told her. "But counterfeiting credit cards is high-tech crime. At least some of the ring members are probably computer whizzes who could easily hack into files on a hard drive. So Graham might have just been playing things safe."

"Or maybe he simply had a gut feeling," Ben suggested. "And everyone knows they aren't always right."

"Like my intuition," Rachel murmured. "I'm go-

ing to have to take it in for an overhaul. I felt sure
it was a dirty cop he was worried about."

As she was speaking, the front door opened and
closed. A moment later, Julie appeared.

"Good news, baby," Chase told her. "The police
arrested the man who killed Graham. We don't have
to worry about them suspecting Rachel anymore."

She raced across the room and gave Rachel a big
hug. Then she flashed Anne such a friendly smile it
warmed her all the way down to her toes.

"Now that you won't have to be helping Rachel
all the time," she said, "can I plot some more of
your book with you? That's really fun."

"I'd love you to. Having a plotting partner's really
fun for me, too."

"You know what?" Chase said to Rachel.

"What?"

"I wouldn't worry about taking your intuition in
for an overhaul. I'd say it's basically in good shape."

"I GUESS WE SHOULD be going, as well," Anne said
once Dave had left.

"Right," her father agreed. "I've got to get some
work done today."

While Rachel was thanking him yet again for his
role in things, Chase quietly said, "I'll bring your
car round to your place in a few minutes."

"Thanks," she murmured.

When he'd driven it home last night, he'd parked
in his driveway. But she could easily get it from there

when she needed it, so bringing it around to her place had to just be an excuse to come over.

Not that she minded. Not even a tiny bit.

After saying goodbye to Rachel and Julie, she headed across the backyard with her father.

As they reached the fence, he said, ''Anne, is there something I should know?''

She glanced at him. ''About what?''

He grinned. ''The way Chase looks at you. And you look at him.''

''Oh. Well…yes, I intended to tell you about that.''

''Tell me? Darling, I'd have to be blind to need telling.''

''Ah.'' She opened the gate and walked the rest of the way to her house, not sure what else to say.

''You haven't known him very long,'' he reminded her once they were inside.

''No,'' she admitted uneasily. ''But we're going to take our time and see how things proceed. I mean, there's Julie to consider. And I've barely moved into this house. I'd hardly—''

''I like him.''

''Well, good,'' she said, suddenly feeling a lot better. ''I'm glad.''

''And I like that he's so close. I was kind of worried about your living in a house alone.''

She smiled. ''You've been doing it for years.''

He didn't smile in return. He merely said, ''Yes …well,'' then cleared his throat.

''Dad? Is everything all right?''

"Everything's fine. It's just that…Anne…I'm seeing someone."

"You mean…a woman?"

"Uh-huh. And…well, I think it's time you met her. How about Saturday?"

She managed to put enough words together to say, "Sure. Saturday's good."

"Okay. I'll call you after I check with her."

"Wait," she said, following along as he headed for the hall. "Aren't you going to tell me about her?"

"Her name's Nancy. She's nice. You'll see for yourself. But I've really got to get going," he added, reaching the front door.

"Dad? Just a second." She closed the distance between them and gave him a hug.

He hugged her back, then said, "See you Saturday," and was out the door.

She stood watching him drive off, feeling a little shell-shocked. It was a good kind of shell-shocked, though, not bad. She liked the idea of his having someone.

She was still standing in the doorway when Chase pulled into the drive.

He got out of the car and started toward her, his smile so sexy that it almost stopped her thinking about her father's news. Almost, but not quite.

"My father has a lady friend," she said.

"Really? Good for him."

"Her name's Nancy."

"Uh-huh."

"He says she's nice."

"So's his daughter."

Chase closed the door, took her in his arms and proceeded to kiss her breathless.

It filled her—utterly and completely—with happiness. He was everything she'd ever dreamed of. Her dreams come true.

"I want to do that for the rest of my life," he murmured at last.

"Only that?" she teased.

He smiled another devastating smile. "Do you have something more in mind?"

She reached for his hand. "Come upstairs and I'll show you."

EPILOGUE

JULIE SAT ON THE LANDING of the back staircase. It was the kind of place Penelope Snow would pick, because she could see most of what was going on in the family room, but no one would notice her and realize it was way past her bedtime.

Scrunching a little closer to the railing, she looked over to where Anne's father and his friend, Nancy, were sitting with Rachel and Dave. Rachel said the two men always had a lot to talk about, 'cuz Anne's father used to be a police detective. But Rachel and Dave must have a lot to talk about, too. If they didn't, they wouldn't be going out together all the time.

After she'd watched them for a minute, her gaze drifted to her father. He was standing in front of the Christmas tree with his arm around Anne.

Their wedding was going to be on New Year's Eve, which wasn't even two weeks away. And her junior bridesmaid's dress was the most beautiful dress in the world. When she'd tried it on to show Daddy, he'd told her she looked like a princess.

Just then, Anne said something that made him laugh—and Julie smiled. He was almost always happy these days. And so was she.

She liked helping Anne with her plotting even

more than she liked helping her dad build his models. So she'd pretty well decided she was going to be a writer when she grew up, instead of a photographer. But she wouldn't tell Rachel that until she decided for sure, in case it hurt her feelings.

Glancing over at her aunt again, she started thinking how strange it was going to seem, after the wedding, when Anne was living here and Rachel was living in Anne's house. But Anne's real estate lady said people should sell houses with pools in the spring or summer. Not in the winter. So Anne was going to wait. And by spring…

Julie turned her attention to Dave. She could tell that he really, really liked Rachel. And if they got married they'd need a house.

She considered that, then smiled again. If she had an aunt and uncle living right behind her and they had a pool, it would be almost as good as convincing Daddy to put one in their yard.

WELCOME TO

If this is your first visit to the
friendly ranching town in the hill
country of Texas, get ready to meet
some unforgettable people. If you've
been there before, you'll be happy to
see some old faces and meet new ones.

Harlequin Superromance® and Margot Dalton—
author of seven books in the original
Crystal Creek series—are pleased to offer
three **brand-new** stories set in Crystal Creek.

IN PLAIN SIGHT by **Margot Dalton**
On sale May 2000

CONSEQUENCES by **Margot Dalton**
On sale July 2000

THE NEWCOMER by **Margot Dalton**
On sale September 2000

HARLEQUIN®
Makes any time special ™

Looking For More Romance?

Visit Romance.net

Look us up on-line at: http://www.romance.net

Check in daily for these and other exciting features:

Hot off the press

View all current titles, and purchase them on-line.

What do the stars have in store for you?

Horoscope

Hot deals

Exclusive offers available only at Romance.net

Plus, don't miss our interactive quizzes, contests and bonus gifts.

PWEB

HARLEQUIN
SUPERROMANCE®

Twins

They're definitely not two of a kind!

THE UNKNOWN SISTER
by
Rebecca Winters

Catherine Casey is an identical twin—and
she doesn't know it! When she meets her
unknown sister, Shannon White, she discovers
they've fallen in love with the same man....

On sale May 2000 wherever Harlequin books are sold.

HARLEQUIN®
Makes any time special ™

HARLEQUIN®
SUPERROMANCE®

*Pregnant and alone—
these stories follow women
from the heartache of
betrayal to finding true love
and starting a family.*

THE FOURTH CHILD by **C.J. Carmichael.**
When Claire's marriage is in trouble, she tries to
save it—although she's not sure she can forgive her
husband's betrayal.
On sale May 2000.

AND BABY MAKES SIX by **Linda Markowiak.**
Jenny suddenly finds herself jobless and pregnant by
a man who doesn't want their child.
On sale June 2000.

MOM'S THE WORD by **Roz Denny Fox.**
After her feckless husband steals her inheritance and
leaves town with another woman, Hayley discovers she's
pregnant.
On sale July 2000.

Available wherever Harlequin books are sold.

HARLEQUIN®
Makes any time special ™

Visit us at www.eHarlequin.com   HSR9ML01